W9-BSC-217

BROKEN GUN

Center Point
Large Print

Also by Wade Everett and available from
Center Point Large Print:

Bullets for the Doctor
Vengeance
The Whiskey Traders

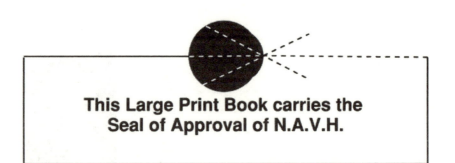

**This Large Print Book carries the
Seal of Approval of N.A.V.H.**

BROKEN GUN

Wade Everett

CENTER POINT LARGE PRINT
THORNDIKE, MAINE

WESTERN
EVE

This Center Point Large Print edition
is published in the year 2017 by arrangement with
Golden West Literary Agency.

Copyright © 1970 by Wade Everett.

All rights reserved.

First US edition: Ballantine Books, Inc.
First UK edition: Hale

The text of this Large Print edition is unabridged.
In other aspects, this book may vary
from the original edition.
Printed in the United States of America
on permanent paper.
Set in 16-point Times New Roman type.

ISBN: 978-1-68324-385-4 (hardcover)
ISBN: 978-1-68324-389-2 (paperback)

Library of Congress Cataloging-in-Publication Data

Names: Everett, Wade, author.
Title: Broken gun / Wade Everett.
Description: Center Point Large Print edition. | Thorndike, Maine : Center Point Large Print, 2017.
Identifiers: LCCN 2017006162| ISBN 9781683243854 (hardcover : alk. paper) | ISBN 9781683243892 (pbk. : alk. paper)
Subjects: LCSH: Large type books. | GSAFD: Western stories.
Classification: LCC PS3553.O5547 B76 2017 | DDC 813/.54—dc23
LC record available at https://lccn.loc.gov/2017006162

CHAPTER 1

As soon as he reached town, Smoke Purcell went to the bank and deposited his pay, keeping out fifteen dollars for what-the-hell money, then he got a bath and a haircut and a shave and new clothes from the skin out and went to the hotel to eat. While he sat there working on his steak and potatoes and stewed tomatoes, he tried to make up his mind whether he liked this or hated it, for it was the same every year, work from early spring until the first snowfall, then get fired for the winter. He even wondered why he came to this town, for it was a week's ride from his home range, but then he supposed it was because of Jim Cardigan; Smoke Purcell always seemed to do what Jim wanted to do.

Winter came early in this high country and from his table near the front window he could see snow packed in the street and piled along the walks and buildings; there'd be more, for this country was always sealed off by winter. Smoke supposed that this was what Jim Cardigan liked about it, the sealed-off feeling it gave him from the troubles of his summers.

And this winter wouldn't be much different from last, Smoke decided, and worked on what was left of his steak. Let's see, he'd been fifteen or twenty minutes in the bank, nearly an hour at the

5

barbershop, and thirty or forty minutes at the store and, reckoning the time for some pie and coffee, another hour here.

It's gettin' about that time, Smoke thought, and waited as he always waited, listening with half an ear to the sounds of the street and the saloon across the way.

A few people came in and went out and some spoke to him for they knew him from other winters. One man stopped at his table and shook hands. "Week late, ain't you Smoke? You usually show up the first week in November."

"Someone else take my job?" Smoke asked.

The man laughed. "Come see me in the morning."

He went out and when he opened the door a wave of cold air came in and the wall lamps flickered briefly. The waiter brought Smoke's pie and some more coffee. He said, "Your friend across the street?"

"He always is, ain't he?" He leaned back in his chair and looked at the waiter. Purcell was a young man, twenty-one or two; he wasn't sure because he was a foundling with no firmly anchored past. He had a thin face and dark brown hair and his eyes were sometimes blue and sometimes a shade of green, while his manner was generally free and easy as though very little bothered him. His habits were his own for his childhood had been brief, and being handed from family to family did not allow him the luxury of family characteristics. He was a man alone in the world, with no past, except what he remembered, and no future, except what he made, and no particular friend, except Jim Cardigan. Maybe that's why he was patient with Jim.

The waiter said, "How long's he been at it now?"

"A couple hours," Smoke said. "It won't be long now."

The waiter laughed. "I never can make up my mind whether he perks up a slow evening or ruins it."

Purcell ate his pie and was working on his third cup of coffee when he heard a man whoop in a high, ringing voice, at which he sighed, got up from the table, laid fifty there, put on his sheepskin coat and went out.

He walked through the snow at the edge of the walk and crossed over and opened the door of the saloon. Jim Cardigan was backed against the bar waving a chair back and forth in his hand while everyone else was backed away from him, wanting to get at him, but afraid to be the first in there. Cardigan was unsteady on his feet for he'd had two hours of drinking behind him and a whole summer of simmering discontent to boil off, and he was swearing, more to himself than to anyone else.

Smoke Purcell edged through the thin crowd, gently forcing men aside until he stood in front of Cardigan, yet out of reach. Cardigan saw him and said, "I don' want to hurt you, Smoke."

7

"Then don't," Purcell said. "Put the chair down, Jim. Let's not have a ruckus."

"Gonna have a big ruckus tonight," Cardigan said. He was a tall man, solid in the way range-bred men are solid, lean and hard and always a little dangerous. He had a dark, brooding air about him, and the liquor brought it out. Cardigan was a good ten years older than Smoke Purcell, but the ten years were only years and a man could sense that when the two were together.

There was a relationship between these two men that others only felt and Cardigan stopped waving the chair and looked at Purcell as though in some secret way he was a little afraid, wanting to hold back, not push anything.

Purcell said, "Jim, do I have to take that away from you?"

"You jus' come ahead, Smoke." He curled his finger and squinted. "You jus' try it and I'll bus' your head wide open."

The bartender licked his lips and said, "Somebody get Mr. Regan. If his place is goin' to get busted up, he at least ought to know about it."

No one really wanted to miss the trouble, but one man weighed it in his mind and did the right thing; he darted out and ran down the street to get the owner.

Smoke Purcell took a side step, hooked another chair on the rung with his foot and kited it across the sawdust toward Cardigan, making the tall man

8

jump. It distracted him a little, but not much and when Smoke jumped him, Cardigan swung and bounced the chair he held off Purcell's back, then they both crashed into the bar with enough force to move it a few inches.

There was a difference in their weight, but the liquor offset the advantage Cardigan had; Purcell battered him a little with his elbows, then flung an arm around his neck and flipped Cardigan over his hip. He hit the sawdust and grunted and Purcell pounced on him, his hand fumbling under Cardigan's coat for the pistol the man liked to wear. He freed it from its holster and tossed it across the room, then Cardigan hit him in the mouth and knocked him back.

They were both getting to their feet when the door was flung open and Fred Kelso came between them. He held them apart with his outstretched arms, and this stopped them; this and the marshal's badge pinned to Kelso's coat.

"I've had a bellyfull of this," Kelso said. "Every damned year." He looked at Jim Cardigan. "You get on down the street to my office and be mighty quick about it."

"Aw, you don' have to get . . ."

Kelso turned to him. "I told you now. You want to be carried?"

Cardigan's glance turned brooding, and color came to his face because he didn't like to be talked to this way by any man, but some inner caution took hold of him and he let his anger fade.

"All right," he said sourly. Then he looked at Smoke. "You had to start it, didn't you? You just couldn't leave me alone, could you?"

"Go on," Kelso said. "Do as I told you!" He stood there while Cardigan turned and shuffled out, then a motion at the men standing around sent them back to their talk and drinking. He took Purcell by the arm and led him to the end of the bar where they wouldn't be overheard. "Didn't I say last year that I wanted no more trouble?"

"You told him that," Purcell said. "I guess he didn't listen."

"He ought to do that," Kelso said, stroking his mustache. "You ought to see to it, for your own good."

"I never give you trouble."

"That's why you can stay, but he goes," Kelso said. "I mean it, Smoke. He clears out of Summit. The town don't need him."

"That's getting kind of tough, ain't it?" Purcell asked. "Hell, Jim just likes to blow off steam. That's natural, ain't it?"

Kelso studied Purcell a moment, then said, "How come you don't let it off?"

"I do," Purcell said. "When a horse throws me, I cuss a blue streak, and now and then I throw rocks and kick a dog if he's handy." He grinned. "Jim's kind of high-strung, like a spirited horse. Come fall, all the little bothers of the year just sort of bust

10

out of him and he's got to get drunk and raise some hell."

Kelso started to speak, then turned his head when the bartender came up, holding Cardigan's pistol by the barrel. "This here got dropped, marshal."

"Thanks," Kelso said and held the gun in his hand. "I'll take yours too while I'm at it."

Purcell shook his head. "It's in my saddlebag at the hotel. I don't have any need to carry it."

"I want to ask you somethin'," Kelso said. "Why do you come here to winter out? It's a couple hundred miles to your home range. Seems that Cheyenne would be a better place to spend a winter. A real lively town."

"Jim likes it here," Purcell said. "He's always talking about settling down and getting a small place of his own around here."

Fred Kelso rolled his eyes and sighed. "That'll be a great day. But I'm not going to lose sleep over it. You're the savin' man, Smoke. How much you got in Harmon's bank? I ask that in a friendly way."

"About eight hundred dollars," Purcell said. "Or a little more. I don't spend much durin' the summer and every winter I got that job at Slater's feed store." He grinned. "One of these days I'll own a place of my own. It's about all a man can look forward to in this world."

"For every hundred men that dream," Kelso said, "there are damned few that do." He stepped away from the bar. "Come on along. Maybe your friend's

11

had a chance to think it over and cool off now."

They went out and down the street to Kelso's office, where Jim Cardigan was standing in front of the potbellied stove, toasting himself. Kelso put Cardigan's gun in the desk drawer and sat down; he looked at Cardigan for a moment before speaking. "Why the hell can't you behave yourself?"

Cardigan shrugged and stood there with his hands thrust deep in his coat pockets. "If I did any damage, I'll pay for it," he said.

"Move on in the morning," Kelso said mildly. He looked steadily at Cardigan whose face slowly reddened. "Don't you think for a minute I don't mean it, Jim. When you get laid off in the fall you can take your trouble somewhere else. I don't need it in Summit. This is sheep country, Jim. You know what that means? Peaceful dogs and peaceful people. Leave it alone."

"I'm an adaptable cuss," Cardigan said, smiling. "Don't a man ever get another chance with you, Kelso?"

"Four years now. This is the last." He took out Cardigan's gun and slid it across the desk. "Stay the night in the hotel. Have a good breakfast, then leave."

Smoke Purcell opened the door and stood there, and presently Cardigan sighed, holstered his pistol and stepped outside. They went across the street together, entered the hotel and, still without a word, walked upstairs. Purcell had the key and he unlocked the door and turned up the lamp, then sat down to pull off his boots.

Finally Cardigan said, "Ain't you ever goin' to speak to me again?"

"I hadn't ought to," Purcell said. "I ought to have let you go and get into it good. Kelso would have thrown you in jail. Maybe that's what you need."

"I've been in jail a couple of times," Cardigan admitted. "Didn't like it. But it never cured anything either." He hung up his coat and stoked the Franklin stove until it put out a good heat. "I guess we'll have to split up," he said. "I couldn't ask you to leave too."

"Go ahead and ask," Purcell said. "I'd like to tell you no."

"It ain't that I'm bad," Cardigan said. "It's just that I've got a restlessness in me that won't quit. We've been together six years now, since you was a sprout. A man gets used to a partner."

"Get used to another one," Purcell said flatly. "I like it here. Maybe I'll stay for good come spring. You never can tell." He flopped on the bed and put his hands behind his head. "Where do you figure on headin'?"

Cardigan shrugged. "I don't know. Until I come to another town I guess. There ought to be someplace in this world where a man can feel—" He stopped and Purcell looked at him.

"Feel what?" Purcell asked.

"Well, like he belonged," Cardigan said. "All

13

my life I've felt loose, like I was somethin' extra, somethin' that wasn't really needed. It bothers me some."

"It don't bother me," Purcell said. "I belong to me, and that's all there is to it." He turned and looked back to the ceiling. "How much money you got?"

"A hundred dollars, more or less," Cardigan said. "It'll carry me to spring."

"If you stay away from cards and booze," Purcell told him. "Can't you save anything?"

"I guess I don't think anything is worth saving," Cardigan said. He opened the stove door and threw in another piece of wood. "A man goes along for years, thinking that not much will change, but I guess it does. You'll be a hard man to say goodbye to, Smoke. I'll miss you."

"You'll get someone else."

Cardigan shook his head. "You've been a real friend."

"You'll get someone else," Purcell said again. "I know that, because you're the kind of man who can't be without somebody. And that's what you got without me, nobody."

"When you say it like that it sounds kind of mean," Cardigan said softly. "We always got along, Smoke. I thought that was good. And you with no folks or anything, I thought we kind of were like brothers. I've always been alone, you know."

"You're goin' to have me cryin' in a minute," Purcell said and turned to face the wall.

14

Jim Cardigan stood there, his dark face full of regret. "Of the two of us," he said, "folks always accepted you and tolerated me. I knew that and I got used to it. I guess it's wrong, my goin' on toots now and then, and fighting when I've had too much to drink. And I'm not a thrifty man like you, Smoke, but in spite of all that I always thought that you saw something in me that you liked, something that you respected, something that held us together through thick and thin."

He stood still, waiting for the answer, waiting to be told what those things might be, but Smoke Purcell didn't speak; he didn't turn and look at Cardigan, and eventually the big man sighed and sat down to take off his boots.

Finally Purcell said, "I'll go with you in the morning and if you thank me, I'll knock your brains out." He reached out and cupped his hand around the lamp chimney and blew it out, bringing darkness into the room.

CHAPTER 2

They ate breakfast in the hotel dining room, and while Jim Cardigan loafed over his coffee, Smoke Purcell left to get their horses, stopping on the way at the bank to draw out his money. Andrew Harmon waited on him personally, counting out the gold, which Purcell put in a small leather sack and hung around his neck.

"Sorry to see you leaving," Harmon said. "I really am. You've been coming back here year after year and I was beginning to think you'd stay on."

"I'd been thinking on it," Purcell said.

"Folks around here would like to see you stay," Harmon said. "You're a steady man with saving ways. That partner of yours is no loss." His plump jowls quivered in agitation. "Purcell, better start to think of yourself. A man's got a right and a duty to himself, you know." He started to reach out and take Purcell by the arm, but thought better of it. "The world's full of boozers and free spenders. When they go down they take their friends with them."

"Nothing's going to change me," Purcell said, buttoning his coat. "I came here with Jim and I'll go with him. What happens after that is anyone's guess."

Harmon smiled and offered his hand. "You're a

16

real man for saying that. And I've got to admire you for it."

"Goodbye," Purcell said and left the bank. He took the horses to the hotel and found Cardigan waiting for him, walking up and down and stamping his feet.

"Look at that sky," Cardigan said. "There's weather making up. I'd like to get twenty or thirty miles beyond the pass before it lets go." He stopped talking as Fred Kelso came toward them, his hands thrust deep in his pockets.

Kelso came up and said, "There's a town called Sunrise about fifty miles east of here. You can make it in three days if you don't waste time." He took his hand out of his pocket and offered it to Cardigan. "No hard feelings? Just doing a job."

Cardigan would have taken it had not Smoke Purcell reached out and batted it aside. "We're going," Purcell said. "Be happy with it."

"No one told *you* to go," Kelso said evenly. Then he shrugged. "You suit yourself."

"I try to," Purcell said and mounted his horse. Cardigan swung up and they rode out of town, taking the east road. This was mountain country, not the eastern kind of mountains, but rocky bastions that reached up into the sky and blocked out the sun two hours before it was due to set. This was a country of faint trails and nearly impassable roads and hidden valleys and deep snows in the winter.

Civilization had just barely touched it. It was a country full of game and deep stands of timber and hardly a telegraph pole anywhere, while a hundred miles away people in Cheyenne had electric lights and telephones and tap water in their kitchens.

They used up that day traveling slowly, but steadily, following what passed as a stage road in good weather, and that night they reached the summit of the pass and from then on it would be downgrade going.

For a campsite they stamped down some snow in a rocky pocket alongside the road, gathered dried brush and built a fire. Cardigan cut some green boughs and spread them thickly on the ground and then laid down his waterproof tarp and blankets while Purcell made the coffee and fried some side meat.

There hadn't been much talk during the day, but then, there never was. While they ate, Cardigan said, "The weather ain't about to hold off much longer."

"What can I do about it?" Purcell asked.

"We ought to find some good cover and weather it out," Cardigan said. "A cave or some timber in the lower reaches."

"If it turns off bad we'll find something."

"The time to get ready is before it hits," Cardigan said. "You burned the meat again."

"I'm no cook. Never said I was," Purcell said. He took out his tobacco and rolled a smoke, then tossed the sack to Cardigan, who never seemed to think of buying these things.

Cardigan sat on his haunches, smoking, his eyes half closed. "You know, now I wish I'd hunted up a woman in Summit instead of hitting the saloon. This is a lonely way to live."

"I never heard you complain much," Purcell said.

"It's just something I never felt like talking about."

"Then why talk about it now?" Purcell asked.

"You're right," Cardigan said and rolled into his blankets.

The cold got them up before it was even daylight and they made only coffee before starting riding again. The snow came later, a light, fine-falling snow; it was late in the day before the flakes became larger, a wind came up and the snow grew thicker.

They were in a valley, a wooded, rolling valley, and Cardigan picked a place for them to stop and Purcell picketed the horses while Cardigan found wood for a fire. It was daylight, but the snowfall cut visibility to a minimum and they could have been a hundred yards from a town without knowing it.

"Goddamned weather," Purcell said as he came back to the fire.

"We ought to have a lean-to," Cardigan said. "No tellin' when this'll let up."

"How far do you think we've come?" Purcell asked.

"Today?"

"Since Summit."

Cardigan thought a moment. "Maybe thirty-five miles. Forty on the outside."

"That town ain't much further then," Purcell said.

"It's too far in this kind of weather," Cardigan said. "One mistake, one slip on the trail and you'd be finished."

Purcell looked at him. "You say, 'you.' You wouldn't make a mistake?"

"I wouldn't make the first mistake," Cardigan said. "And that would be stirring from here until this clears up."

"It's a hell of a way to spend the winter," Purcell said, and got out the coffee and pot while Cardigan melted snow to make the biscuits.

By nightfall, Cardigan had built a crude lean-to, cleared away the snow beneath it and covered the ground with boughs. It was a shelter and that was all, but the fire at the open front of it threw heat into it, for he had banked it with two hunks of deadfall.

"Snug," Cardigan said.

"The hotel in Summit was snug," Purcell said.

An irritation came into Cardigan's expression. "Ain't I ever gonna hear the last of that?"

"You may just never," Purcell said.

"I'd like to have a job that lasted all year," Cardigan said. "Maybe we ought to try to get a job working for the railroad in the spring."

20

"What do you know about the railroad?"

"Well, I mean, in the stockyards somewhere?"

"I don't know what I'll do in the spring," Purcell said. "I know I'm not going back to working cattle for Roberts." He said it easy, as though he hadn't thought much about it, but Cardigan wasn't fooled.

He looked intently at Purcell and said, "You never said anythin' to me about this."

"Do I have to tell you everything? Hell, what am I, your brother or somethin'?"

Cardigan opened his mouth to say something, then stopped and held up his hand. "I heard somethin'." He sat with his mouth open, breathing silently, his head cocked to one side. "There it is. You hear it?"

"It's the wind," Purcell said.

"No wind. That was a horse screaming." He got up quickly and cracked his head on the cross-pole of the lean-to.

"Where the hell you going?" Purcell asked.

"To saddle up," Cardigan said, not looking back.

Purcell hesitated, then cursed under his breath and followed Cardigan as though he were accustomed to catering to this man's whims. Cardigan had the blanket on and swung the saddle up and was soon ready to go back and roll his gear. Purcell hurried but he was only lashing his bedroll on when Cardigan mounted and started out.

He had an ear and a sense of direction that couldn't be faulted and Purcell relied on it, kicking his horse into motion so as not to lose sight of Cardigan; if he did he'd never find his way, not even back to the lean-to.

They rode for what seemed a very long time, Cardigan stopping often to listen. If he heard anything, he never spoke of it; Purcell heard nothing at all. But Cardigan seemed to hear enough to keep him pushing on, until ahead and a little to the left, a rosy glow appeared in the snow.

"Fire," Cardigan said. "Someone's gettin' burned out!"

They rode on and were brought up by a fence; instead of hunting for the gate, Cardigan kicked down two rails and jumped his horse through the gap.

They were in a ranch yard; the barn was gone, as were most of the outbuildings, while only a thick pad of snow on the cabin roof kept sparks from burning that too. Cardigan flung himself off his horse and ran toward the barn and suddenly fell full-length in the snow. He swore, hating his own clumsiness, then saw by the flickering red light that he had stumbled over someone.

"Over here!" he yelled, and as Smoke Purcell came up, Cardigan peered closer and saw that it was a woman. "Give me a hand," he said and started to lift her.

They carried her into the cabin and Purcell struck matches until he found a lamp. Cardigan put her on the floor near the fireplace and Purcell touched off some shavings and got a fire going.

"It's funny," he said, "to be lighting a fire inside and being burned out by one outside."

"Shut up," Cardigan said.

His eyes were adjusting to the light and he saw that the woman was young, in her middle twenties, and barefoot, wearing only a long sheepskin coat over her nightgown.

Purcell found another lamp and put a match to it, then went into the other two rooms and took a look around. He came back and said, "A man lives here. He has got a room and so has she. Either they're family or else married and not . . ."

"Go outside and see what you can do," Cardigan said, his tone curt. "Well, go on. Maybe he's hurt somewhere."

"Why don't you go out and I'll—" Smoke stopped talking and grinned. "All right, I'll go." He closed the door and Cardigan took off his heavy gloves and began briskly rubbing the woman's feet and ankles. He was a little embarrassed at having to do this, but there was no telling how long she had been standing out there in the snow up to her knees and he knew that he had to get the circulation going.

The fire was putting out a respectable heat now and he turned her so that her feet were closer to it, and went on rubbing. She moaned and then cried out in pain and he knew that he was getting somewhere; when it hurt, frostbite was licked.

She opened her eyes and turned her head and looked at him and he got up and went to a cupboard and opened and slammed doors until he found a whiskey bottle and some glasses and poured a stiff drink, then held her half sitting and forced her to take it. She choked and tried to spit but he clamped a hand over her mouth until she swallowed, then he laid her back down again.

Her feet were really hurting and she kept drawing them under her and moaning softly and he made her straighten them out and rubbed them some more, and then Smoke Purcell came in and closed the door.

"He never made it out of the barn," Purcell said. "Who is she?"

"How do I know?" Cardigan said.

"Ask her."

"Ask her next week or next year, but not now," Cardigan said. "Get a blanket and a pillow out of the bedroom."

When Purcell brought them, he wrapped her well and tucked the pillow under her head. The whiskey put a glow in her cheeks and she watched him, never taking her eyes off his face.

Finally she said, "He's in the barn. A timber fell on him."

"We know, lady," Purcell said. "He your husband?"

"Leave her alone," Cardigan said.

"I only asked a question." He came over and

squatted so she could see him without turning her head. And he smiled and his face was young and good and the smile reached her where words could not so that they were no longer strangers. "I'm Smoke Purcell," he said. "This is my pardner, Jim Cardigan. We saw the fire, but got here too late. I'm sure sorry."

"The horse woke us," she said. "He was screaming, trapped in the barn. It was the hay, I guess. Got a little wet last year."

"You shouldn't talk now," Purcell said gently. "Can you make it to your bed, lady? We'll keep a fire going and if you want to just talk to someone, we'll be here."

"Yes," she said. "You're kind."

Cardigan would have helped her up, but Purcell just eased himself in and put his arm gently around her. It wasn't a fresh thing to do, and she was grateful for the help; he took her to the door and let her go the rest of the way herself, telling her only before she closed the door, "I'd cry. There's nothin' like it."

Then, once the door was closed, he got the coffeepot and put it near the fire and got some cold meat and sliced it. Cardigan stood there, back to the fire, watching him. "You just go ahead and help yourself, Smoke," he said.

"Hell, no one will mind, Jim. Fix you a sandwich?"

Cardigan shook his head. "You know how to talk to a woman."

25

"There's nothin' to it," Purcell said, coming back to the fire with his sandwich. He smiled. "You look pretty down at the mouth, Jim. Cheer up. That lean-to would have got pretty cold before morning."

"A man died out there tonight," Cardigan said softly. "Died hard."

"Did you know him?"

"You know I didn't," Cardigan said testily.

"Then what are you fretting about?" Purcell said. "Look, I don't mean that to sound tough, but you think about it. You can't cry for everybody, Jim. Every stray dog and cat you've got to feel sorry for."

"I felt sorry for you once," Cardigan said easily. "What do you have to say about that?"

"What do you want me to say?" Purcell asked. "Go on, make yourself a sandwich. You're as hungry as I am and the roast's pretty good."

CHAPTER 3

Toward morning the storm broke and the silence woke Jim Cardigan with a start; he got up and built up the fire to drive the cold from the room. His activity woke Smoke Purcell, who was sleeping nearby.

"What's goin' on?" Purcell asked, sitting up. Cardigan was chucking wood into the cookstove and the only light in the room was what was cast through the window.

"The storm's over," Cardigan said. "No wind." He went to the door and opened it and saw that the snow had stopped falling. He closed it and went back to poke the fire. "We'll dig a grave as soon as it's light. I don't want her to see him, burned like that."

"I don't want to see him either," Smoke said. "Put on the coffee if there's any left."

Cardigan hefted the pot, swished it around and decided there was enough and put it on the stove to heat. "I didn't sleep good. Did you?"

"I always sleep good," Smoke said. "That's because I'm pure in heart. Now you're probably thinking about all the women you've fooled around with and all the . . ."

"Don't start that," Cardigan said. He leaned against the wall by the stove and darkness hid his expression, but the run of his voice was soft, tinged with regret. "When you get my age, Smoke, you think of a woman, and a home. Runnin' around don't seem as much fun as it did. You get to lookin' at women different, that's all."

"I wouldn't look in dance halls and some of those back street houses," Smoke Purcell said.

"Yeah," Cardigan said. "But it depends on what you've got to offer a woman, boy. A man's got to be worthy of a good woman." He sighed and moved to the table and lit the lamp, keeping it turned down low. Then he rolled a cigarette and bent over the glass chimney for his light, standing there until the rising heat ignited the tobacco. He puffed and blew some smoke down inside the chimney and it turned milky, then brown, then faded completely. Cardigan's angular face was harsh, a face life had used and left with lines around the mouth and eyes. His nose was a hard ridge, too thin, too finely pointed, and his lips were mostly tight-drawn and half hidden by his full mustache. It was the kind of face a man could look at and tell that here was a man without much resistance to anything, good or bad, a man who drank and caroused and fought and was sorry afterward, but not sorry enough to keep from doing it again. It was the kind of face a salesman could look at and know that he could score with that old merchandise he hadn't been able to get rid of. It was the kind of a face a gambler liked because he could run his bluffs without much danger of being called. Yet it was the kind of face an employer looked for when he hired, for in Cardigan's eyes there was a steadiness, an honesty that men could rely on.

"How many years have you ridden for old man Paulson?" Smoke asked.

Cardigan thought a moment. "Over ten, I guess. Yes, nearly eleven."

"And you made four hundred a year and found," Smoke said. "If you'd spent a hundred of that and salted the rest, you'd have over three thousand dollars now. With that kind of money you could be ranching your own place and courtin' a decent woman in a Sears buggy." He threw off his blankets and pulled on his boots. "I don't feel sorry for you, Jim. Not a bit."

The coffee was hot and Cardigan got a couple of cups from the sink drainboard and filled them. He left one sitting there and Smoke Purcell got up and came after it. Then Cardigan said, "I guess I'd better look in on her, huh?"

"I'll do that," Purcell said. "Your idea of talking to a woman is patting her on the flank and asking how much."

"Oh, hell now," Cardigan said, but Purcell was already stepping to the door. He did not knock, just opened it slowly and stood quiet, looking into the dim room. The bed made a faint noise as the woman turned and raised up and Purcell said, "I made you some coffee, ma'am. You want me to leave it or do you feel like comin' out? There's a fire goin' and . . ."

"I'll come out," she said and got up, slipping into her robe. In a minute or two she stepped into the main room and the lamplight struck her full and soft. She was taller than most women and quite slender and her face was more square than oval. Crying had puffed her eyes, but Cardigan, studying her, could see that she was through with that now. He pulled a chair away from the table and she sat down, glancing at him, thanking him as she sat.

"The storm's broke," Cardigan said.

She seemed to notice then and nodded. "That's good." She lifted the coffee cup Purcell had given her and sipped at it, then put it down and sat with her hands cupped around it. "My name's Lila Ramey. I guess I didn't tell you. I'm sorry." She turned her head and looked at Smoke Purcell. "My half brother, Paul . . ."

"Now don't you worry none about that," Purcell said. "I was just tellin' Jim, before you woke up, that we'd take care of the buryin'. If there's any special place . . ."

She shook her head. "No, he never thought about dying. I guess none of us do."

"Did your brother work this place alone?" Cardigan asked.

"Yes. There's five hundred acres and we used some of the government land, along with the neighbors." She turned her head toward him. "You're not a sheep man, are you?"

"Cattle," he said. "Although I know about 'em."

"Animals have to be taken care of," Smoke Purcell said. "Come rain or shine or bad luck, they've got to be tended. I know this is a bad time to talk of it, but we'd be willin' to stay on and work your critters until you can make up your mind what you want to do."

Jim Cardigan said, "Now wait a minute, Smoke."

"I've decided," Purcell said. "Go on if you want to."

"Don't see no sense in doin' that," Cardigan said. "But we're not sheep men, Smoke. All we know about 'em is what we've picked up secondhand. It just seems that we ought to give this some thought before we decide."

"I told you I'd decided," Purcell said. "Providin' it's all right with Miss Ramey."

"How can I be anything but grateful?" Lila said. "Of course I'll pay you if the storm hasn't wiped me out."

"There's plenty of time to talk about that," Smoke Purcell said, picking up his coat. "It's about to get light. Jim and I'll tend to things. You ought to lay down and get some more rest." He stepped to the door and nodded for Jim Cardigan to get his coat, then went out.

Lila Ramey said, "He's a stubborn man, isn't he?"

31

"Mighty set in his ways," Cardigan agreed and put on his coat.

"But they're good ways," Lila said. "That's what really counts, isn't it?"

"You could say that," Cardigan said and went outside.

The air was cold and biting, but there was no wind and the sky was clear and snow was blown into drifts and long windrows. Purcell was digging around a half-burned tool shed and found a pick and a shovel with handles somewhat charred. He handed the pick to Cardigan and said, "These'll do if we're careful not to break 'em."

"Have you dug around the rubble yet?"

"We'll bury him where he is," Purcell said. "Better that way."

"I guess you always know what's best," Cardigan said.

Purcell looked at him sharply. "What's that mean?"

"You were doin' a lot of talkin' in there, and a lot of decidin'."

"So that's eatin' you, is it?" He smiled and slapped Cardigan on the shoulder. "You know how I hate explainin' things. It was just to save time. All right?"

"Sure," Cardigan said after a brief hesitation. "Let's get at it."

They worked for three hours to dig a foot and a half, then they got past the frost and it went faster and finally they had the grave ready. It made Cardigan a little sick to think of it, but one had to be practical about these things and they dug only a four-by-four-by-two-hole because Ramey was so badly burned that he wouldn't need one any larger. And they didn't bother with a blanket or anything, just pushed what was left into the grave with some charred boards and hurriedly covered it up.

Purcell was tapping the mound with the shovel when Cardigan touched him on the shoulder and he turned to see three men coming toward the burned ruins. They were afoot, on snowshoes, and they quickened their pace when they came into the yard, as though they wanted to run this last distance and were held back only by great personal restraint.

"Neighbors more than likely," Purcell said and cast the shovel aside and walked out to meet them. For a moment they just stood there and looked at each other, then the oldest of the three said, "Be that Paul Ramey you've buried there?"

"Yes," Purcell said. "You knew him?"

"Been his neighbors," the man said. "I be Clyde Means. This here's Mort Denny and his boy, Asa." They bobbed heads in acknowledgment, then waited for either Cardigan or Purcell to say something.

"We heard some noise and came here durin' the storm," Cardigan said. "Too late though. Ramey was dead and his sister was in the yard. She's all right now, if there is an all right after a thing like this."

"Some timbers let go and fell on him," Purcell said. "I don't guess he suffered any."

"You've done a Christian thing," Mort Denny said. He was a small man, even bundled in a sheepskin coat. "It might not hurt none if I said somethin' over the grave. Everybody around here knows I read the Book all the time."

"You go right ahead," Purcell said. "If you've got no objections, I'll stand with you." He looked at the others. "I guess we're all godly men."

"Bless you, brother," Denny said and led the way to the newly covered grave. He took off his hat, then said, "Maybe the sister would like to join us and . . ."

"She has cried enough," Cardigan said flatly.

"Perhaps you're right," Denny said. He looked at the others and they remembered their hats. Then he said, "Oh, Lord, we give into your keeping a sinner. Paul Ramey was a man with a lust for high livin' and a pretty ankle. But he tended his flock, oh Lord. Show him your mercy because he went suddenlike, with no chance to atone for his sins."

Cardigan said, "Ain't you got nothin' good to say about him? Didn't he have a nice head of hair or somethin'?"

"You're interruptin' me," Denny said, a testiness in his voice.

"Yeah, be quiet," Purcell said. "There's no need to offend this man. Go on, Mr. Denny."

"Thank you, son. There's good in you." He looked at the sky. "Pass this man through, oh Lord. I ask it as a favor, from your servant, Morton T. Denny." He clapped his hat on his head. "That ought to shoot him through proper." He smiled and showed some missing teeth. "I do most of the prayin' in the valley. That was my two-dollar send off, but I don't intend to bother the bereaved woman at this time about it."

"Decent of you," Cardigan said.

"I know that," Denny said sincerely. "I'm a decent man."

"How come you gents showed up this mornin'?" Purcell asked. "Did you know somethin' was wrong?"

"Paul, he didn't come to town last night," Clyde Means said. "Never knew Paul to miss his Saturday-night poker." He looked from Purcell to Cardigan and back. "This is Sunday, you know."

"We didn't know," Cardigan said. "Kind of lost track of time, I guess. You gents want to talk to Miss Ramey?"

"No need of it now," Denny said. "Later though. She can't run this place by herself. Best to sell it."

"We're goin' to be around awhile," Cardigan said.

Their eyebrows went up. Means said, "You're strangers."

35

"So?" Purcell said.

"Well, I mean, none of us know you," Denny said.

"As long as the sheep don't mind," Cardigan said, "why should you?" He looked at Asa Denny, a grown man. "Don't he talk?"

"I talk for him," Mort Denny said. "He stays out of trouble that way."

"Now that you know what happened," Purcell said, "I guess you'll tell it around the valley and maybe next week you'll all come over and help us put up new buildings."

"Hadn't considered it," Denny said.

"Do consider it," Cardigan said bluntly.

"You just said how decent you was," Purcell said. "And we appreciate it. Suppose you make it five days from now. That would be Friday. We'll have the logs cut by then. Bring your friends."

Denny and Means looked at each other, then nodded. Means said, "I guess the stock scattered, huh? Paul had some horses and two cows."

"We'll find 'em," Cardigan said. "Where do the sheep go when the weather turns foul?"

Mort Denny pointed to the high country on the other side of the valley. "The wind keeps the snow clear in the high meadows. They graze there all winter long. Government land. We all use it."

"Your flock up there?" Purcell asked.

"Yep," Means said.

"If those sheep are all mixed up, how do you tell 'em apart?" Purcell asked.

Means looked at Denny, then said, "Why, I guess you just got to know 'em on sight." He drew on his mittens. "Let's get back, Mort, Asa. Been away too long now. See you fellas Friday."

"Sure," Purcell said and they stood there while the three men left the yard. Cardigan opened his mouth to speak but Purcell shook his head and said softly, "Voices carry a long way in this cold." He waited a few minutes, then laughed.

"What's so funny?" Cardigan asked. "And what's that bull about recognizin' your own flock. You know they all got a bell sheep with a different bell."

"Yeah, but they didn't know we knew it," Purcell said. "Real decent people, huh? Before the day's out they'll be headin' for the high country to thin out the flock. All right, we'll get there first. Let's go in the cabin."

CHAPTER 4

Smoke Purcell saddled his horse and rode out of the yard ten minutes after Means and the Dennys disappeared from sight, and he headed toward the high country alone. Jim Cardigan watched him go, then went into the cabin and closed the door.

He would rather have gone, and he had argued with Purcell about it, but the younger man would have none of it; he'd asked Lila about the bell, taken his pistol from his saddlebag, and left.

The damned fool will get lost, Cardigan thought and started to fix something to eat. The smell of frying potatoes brought Lila Ramey from her room. She was dressed except for shoes, and when Cardigan looked at her stockinged feet, she said, "They hurt. I suppose I got a touch of frostbite."

"Wouldn't surprise me none," he said.

She came to the stove and stood there a moment, then gently put him out of the way. "Cooking is a woman's job."

"I was only trying to . . ."

"I know," she said. "But I'll do it. Go sit down."

He hesitated, then went to the table and pulled back a chair. Then he rolled a cigarette and smoked and watched her work. She was through with grief, and it was a good thing, he reasoned. Sometimes there wasn't time or even a place for it.

When the meal was ready, she brought it to the table and he waited for her to sit down, then picked up his knife and fork. "I don't suppose you know how the fire started," he said.

Lila Ramey shook her head. "Paul woke first and went out. No, I don't know. I only know that it couldn't have come at a worse time. We sold off nearly half the flock to pay debts. But Paul still owes money in town. I don't know how much. He never told me."

"That wasn't smart," Cardigan said. "I notice that there don't seem to be anythin' new around here. Been a long time since anythin's been done. I ain't sayin' that to be criticizin', you understand. It's just that there's always somethin' goin' to pot on a place, a fence or a roof or somethin'. All the time you've got to be fixin' and buildin' or it just falls down on you."

"This was my father's place," Lila said. "Paul was never much for sheep ranching, but when pa died, he had to take it over. Gave up a town job to do it and somehow it's been going downhill."

"Is this all that's left to you?"

"Yes, but I can't keep it. Paul owed money and—" She shrugged and went on eating. "Why worry about it now? As soon as the news gets out, creditors will be showing up with a bill in their hand." She forced a smile to her face; she hadn't much to smile about. "Your ham's getting cold," she said. "And it isn't your trouble."

Purcell's horse was rested and he spent two hours bucking drifted snow before he worked his way into the higher country where the wind had swept patches clear. He followed a natural trail upward until the valley lay almost in full view below him. Here was a land of small meadows, snow-covered in spots, but blown clean by the fierce winter winds in areas exposed to the northeast.

He found flocks of sheep, and dogs who came barking and running toward him, but they were friendly dogs who, after sniffing at his horse, went back to work. To his untrained ear, the sounds of one bell sheep sounded like any other, which irritated him. To have come here to be stopped by such a small thing!

The bell he listened for was high-pitched, higher than any other, yet he could not pick it out. A look at the sky told him that there wasn't much daylight left, so he searched about for a campsite and decided on a place in a high rocky pocket cut off by bare walls on three sides. He gathered brush for his fire and built it up well, then cooked some bacon in the small frying pan he had also taken from his saddlebag.

While he was eating, a huge sheep dog came into his camp, wagging his tail. His fur was long and matted and he was black-and-white with a star on the muzzle, and Purcell grinned, snapped his fingers, and said, "Here, Buck."

The dog came to him then and he rubbed his ears

and patted the animal on the head and laughed. Lila had mentioned the dog—the color of him, his name—and Purcell figured that this would take the place of any bell sheep. In the morning, the dog would point out the flock to him easy enough.

Purcell had eaten his meat and was melting snow in the skillet for his coffee when the dog perked up his ears in the direction of the darkness beyond the rim of the firelight. Purcell listened a moment, then heard a horse snort and a man say something, and he bent forward and put his hand under his coat and touched the cold butt of his pistol. He slid it out of the holster and laid it on his thigh and covered it with the tail of his coat.

Then he finished making his coffee; by the time it came to a boil, Means and four other men were dismounting just at the firelight's edge.

"Didn't expect to find anyone here," Means said. "You know Denny and his boy." He turned to another man. "This is Joe Harms and Ray Kline. That coffee smells good."

"There's enough to go around," Purcell said. "You saw the fire?"

"Couldn't miss it from the meadow," Means said. He looked at the others. "We came up to look at our flock."

"I already looked at mine," Purcell said casually.

Mort Denny said, "Thought you couldn't tell . . ."

"I learned," Purcell said and smiled. He glanced at Joe Harms and Ray Kline and saw that they were armed, Kline with a shotgun and Harms with a rifle. "Expect to shoot somethin'?" he asked.

"You never know," Kline said dryly.

"I always figure that way myself," Purcell said and leaned forward to take the skillet off the fire. He used the corner of his coat to prevent burning his hand and casually displayed the .45 resting on his thigh. He did not touch the pistol or look at it, but the others saw it and if they had been considering surprising anyone, they changed their plans. Purcell put the frying pan on the ground and said, "Help yourselves." Then he smiled at them. "Yes, sir, if anyone was to come up here and figure on adding to their flock just because a poor, out-of-work cowboy didn't know too much about sheep, they'd likely pick up a few bullet holes. Now don't you gents think that's about right?"

They nodded and murmured and looked at each other.

"So I said to myself this afternoon, 'Smoke Purcell, you ought to ride up there just in case some lowdown thieves show up to take advantage of a poor woman's troubles.'" He spread his hand . "And here I am and here you are, both thinkin' the same thing. Ain't that a coincidence?"

"It sure is," Mort Denny said. "Ain't that so, Harms?"

"Maybe it is and maybe it ain't," Harms said. "I'm not scared much."

"What's to be scared of?" Purcell said in a

friendly tone. "Of course, if you so much as raise the muzzle of that rifle one inch I'd blow you to kingdom come." He said it without the slightest change of tone and looked steadily at them while he talked, the smile never leaving his face.

"My aim's not too good," Ray Kline said. "That's why I carry a shotgun." He stood there, cradling it in his arm, watching Smoke Purcell.

Then Purcell said, "Break it open and throw the shells on the ground." He saw the stubborn resistance come into Kline's long face. "Friend, I won't tell you again."

Kline didn't have the nerve and Purcell sensed it. Finally the man took off his glove, broke open the shotgun and let the shells drop. Purcell looked at Joe Harms. "What are you thinkin' about?"

"I'm not thinkin' about a thing," Harms said. He realized what Purcell was talking about, what he was waiting for, and slowly placed the rifle against a rock and put his hands in his coat pockets.

"Now I want to tell you gents somethin'," Purcell said. "I'm goin' to run the place for Miss Lila, and I'm goin' to run it some different than it's been run in the past. Bein' a cattleman, I like lots of room, 'cause you never can tell how much I'll want to expand. This tableland is government property. I suggest you pull off it. And don't take too long in doin' it."

"We've been usin' this graze for years," Denny said hotly. "That's not fair, one man hoggin' it."

"You want to fight for it?" Purcell asked.

Clyde Means said, "What you mean, fight?"

"It's open country," Purcell said. "It's free for the takin' to any man willin' to hold it. I'm willin' to go to a little trouble to do it. Like shootin' somebody if I have to."

"People don't do things like that no more," Kline said. He laughed uneasily. "Why, we're civilized people. We've got laws."

"You want to yell for the law?" Purcell asked. He laughed. "Go ahead and yell if you think anyone will hear you. Now I told you what I'm goin' to do. I'll give you ten days to do it."

"And if we don't?" Kline asked.

"You'll need your shotgun," Purcell said flatly. "You figured to pick out some lambs for yourselves, didn't you? Somethin' for nothin'. Then why shouldn't I have somethin' for nothin'?" He leaned back and smiled at them. "It has been a mean winter. Likely it'll get worse."

"That's a fact," Denny said.

"Predators have probably thinned you out some."

"They have," Kline said. "We may do well to break even this year." He squinted at Smoke Purcell. "How can you be sure what we come here for?"

"Because there's no such a thing as an honest man," Purcell said.

They looked at each other, then Kline said, "You know, we ought to be able to talk business with one another. Next Saturday, in town, why don't we sit down over a drink and talk this out?"

"All right," Purcell said. "In the meantime, start cleaning out this high country."

Temper came into Kline's eyes. "Damn it, I thought . . ."

"We're just goin' to talk," Purcell said. "Maybe I'll change my mind then, and maybe I won't."

"There's nothin' to be gained here," Denny said.

They agreed to that and turned to their horses. Purcell sat by his fire while they started to ride out, and then he sprang away to the cover of the nearest rocks, the dog bounding with him, and none too soon, for Kline had reloaded his shotgun and sprayed both barrels into the campfire, thinking he was going to catch Purcell off guard.

From the darkness and his cover, Smoke Purcell laughed and said, "Kline, I thought you were smarter than that! Didn't I just say there wasn't anyone you could trust?"

He heard them riding out then, and he waited a moment, then kicked out the fire and got his horse. The dog trotted along with him for a brief distance, then swung back to the flock, training stronger than this new friendship.

Purcell had no trouble finding his way down out of the high country and he wasn't worried about being waylaid along the trail for Kline knew that he wasn't tangling with a spring chicken, and Joe

Harms just didn't have the guts to shoot it out with anyone.

Dawn found him wearily bucking drifts a mile from the Ramey place, then he saw a lamp go on and used this as a beacon to make the yard. Jim Cardigan surprised him by coming around the side of the cabin, and Purcell dismounted.

"You sleep out?"

"I thought it was proper," Cardigan said stiffly. "We were alone and . . ."

"You're a jackass," Purcell said and stripped the saddle off his horse. He rubbed him down with the blanket, then covered him and led him off. When he came back, Cardigan was waiting by the door, stamping his feet and blowing on his hands.

They went in together and Lila turned from the stove. "I was beginning to worry," she said.

"Never worry about me," Purcell said and smiled. He had a growth of whiskers on his face, but it did not lessen the boyishness, or the impression of youthful honesty that was always there.

"You want to use my razor?" Cardigan asked. He turned to his saddlebags in the corner. "Have any company?"

"Some," Purcell said. He took the razor and went to the sink and Lila brought hot water and a clean towel. While he lathered, he said, "Does Kline or any of the others lease that government land?"

"No," Lila said. "We just use it."

"Then I guess I'll go to town," Purcell said. He

bladed his face clean and held a wet cloth over his eyes for a moment.

"Did you get any sleep at all?" Cardigan asked. Purcell shook his head. "Then I'll go. What do you want done?"

"I want to file for grazing rights," Purcell said. He hung the towel and got a cup and poured some coffee, then took it to the table and sat down. "Your stepbrother must have been an easy man."

"He never liked trouble," Lila said evenly. "Who does?"

"Put it another way," Purcell said. "Who doesn't have trouble?"

"We're gettin' into somethin' that's none of our business," Cardigan said. He glanced at Lila Ramey. "I don't know how to say this, but we're not permanent kind of fellas. In the spring . . ."

"Spring's a long way off," Purcell said. "Jim, you're a nice guy, but I wouldn't give two whoops in hell for your future. Lazy you ain't, but shiftless you are."

"You don't have to talk like that in front of Miss Lila," Cardigan said.

"She's goin' to find it out sooner or later," Purcell said. He pointed to Cardigan. "You and I have been together for some time, and you know good and well that if it wasn't for me steerin' you out of trouble that you'd be holdin' up some bar someplace right now." He blew out a long breath. "You're a tough man, Jim, but you've got no

47

backbone in some things. Now you let me do the decidin' for both of us, or you can saddle up and go your own way now."

Cardigan was angry, but he held it back. Purcell and Lila Ramey watched him as he let the anger leak away and said, "Damn you for being so right all the time." Then he got up, grabbed his coat and went out.

Lila said, "That was a hard thing, Smoke. You hurt him."

"I know," he said. "But every now and then I've got to do that to save him from himself. He just has no aim in life. None at all."

CHAPTER 5

Smoke Purcell took Jim Cardigan's horse because it was fresh, and as he switched saddles, he explained to Cardigan what he wanted done. "I'll spend the night in town. Want to put my money in the bank and tend to a few other things. You can clean up as much of the mess around the barn as you can. The stone foundations are all right and we'll build a new one on the same site." He gave the cinch a final pull and stepped into the saddle. "If I was you I'd sleep outside. Likely some of the neighbor women will be coming over to see what they can do and we wouldn't want to embarrass Lila none, now would we?"

"Don't I get credit for having any sense at all?"

Smoke Purcell laughed and slapped Cardigan on the shoulder. "I was just remindin' you. Ain't you reminded me from time to time? What the hell, Jim, we're partners. Right down the line." Then he kicked the horse into motion and rode out.

Cardigan watched him go, then walked over to the rubble of the burned barn and savagely began to work. Twenty minutes with a shovel worked up his sweat and got the wind in him going deep and steady, and he did not stop, neither to smoke nor rest. He cleared the rubble, starting at the southwest corner, and shoveled it into a huge pile, and while he worked he let his anger simmer away and tried to find the source of it. He didn't like it when Purcell pointed out his weaknesses, and he liked having those weaknesses even less.

He had always figured that he was about the same as most men he knew, neither good nor bad, not worth much but at the same time not worthless. He'd had enough schooling to learn to read and write and do some arithmetic, and after that, he figured, any more was a waste of time for even as a child he realized that he lacked the ambition to use knowledge. So he became like many men, content to work cattle, or the land, or dig in the earth for someone else, and every month he was paid and every month he spent most of it foolishly because he simply didn't have any good reason for doing otherwise.

Smoke was always at him for drinking it up after payday. Hell, what was a man going to do with himself? Lay around the bunkhouse? When he went to town, he was as lonesome there as on the job, and he never knew quite what to say to a decent woman, so courting didn't take up any of his time. So he'd drink and play cards and sometimes win and in the end always lose and there were times when he didn't like paydays at all.

At noon, Lila came to the doorway and stood there, looking at him, expecting him to stop his work, but Cardigan did not and finally she got tired of standing there, tired of waiting, and went back inside. Later she came out with two sandwiches and a cup of coffee and he had to stop, for she stood there holding them.

"Are you going to get it done all in one day?" she asked.

"I wouldn't want to disappoint Smoke," he said. "He disappoints easy."

"You're a strange pair," she said. "Not the same at all."

"Maybe that's what makes us a pair," he said. His glance went past her and held and she turned and saw some women coming into the yard. They wore heavy coats and overshoes that made walking clumsy and were followed by a brood of noisy children who darted about, pelting each other with snowballs.

"The neighbor ladies," Lila said softly, then smiled as they came up. "How are you, Mrs. Means, Mrs. Denny? You brought the children. How nice."

They nodded and the other two, whom Cardigan suspected were the wives of Harms and Kline, looked around.

Mrs. Denny said, "My husband tells me you've got two new men on the place. Where's the other one?"

"He went to town," Lila said pleasantly. "Won't you come in? You must be cold after your walk."

"No need to tramp snow in your place," Mrs. Means said. She was as thin as a cracker and she struck Cardigan as being completely humorless.

"Too bad," she said. "Just too bad. But these things happen. I was tellin' Clyde this mornin' that we just don't know what'll happen to us or how a thing will turn out." She looked at her brood; they were scattered, running about, poking into everything. "They won't bother nothin', will they?" She made a question of it, but her tone plainly indicated that she didn't want an answer. Her glance came to Jim Cardigan. "You don't say much, do you?"

"Didn't want to interrupt," he said.

She frowned easily. "You gettin' sassy with me?"

Lila quickly said, "I've just made coffee. Are you sure you won't have some?" She took Mrs. Denny by the arm and in that way steered them into the cabin where she quickly put out cups and poured the coffee.

Mrs. Means said, "He certainly is a mean-looking man."

"Who?" Lila asked.

"Why, the one outside. I hope you keep your door locked at night. I don't trust any man out of my sight." Hearing the children grow shriller, she went to the door and yelled, "Edgar, you behave yourself now!" Then she came back to the table. "My, they're so spirited, aren't they?"

"I suppose you'll be selling this place now," Mrs. Denny said.

"Well, I hadn't thought about it," Lila confessed.

"It's a reasonable thing to think," Mrs. Means

52

said. "Your brother kind of let things go to pot and like my husband says, you might find it too late to save the place."

Lila Ramey crossed her arms and looked at them. "You're all warmhearted, generous people, aren't you? It kind of chokes me up when I think of it."

"There's no need to carry on like that," Mrs. Denny said and the others nodded. "The truth's got to come out."

"Yes, it does," Lila said. She went to the door and opened it. "Now I'm going to tell you the truth. You're a bunch of old biddies who never have enough trouble of your own so you come over here and poke your nose in mine. Now you get out of my house and off my land and don't you ever come back."

"Well!" Mrs. Means said and compressed her lips into a harsh line. "Come, ladies." She got up and started for the door, then stopped as one of the children began to yell at the top of his lungs. Rushing out, she saw Jim Cardigan with Edgar bent over his knee, whacking his exposed bottom with the flat of his hand while the other children danced around and yelled.

As the rest of the women hurried her way, Mrs. Means tried to grab Cardigan, but he shoved her and she sat down suddenly in the snow. He finished his spanking and Edgar hopped around the yard, his pants and underwear around his ankles, cherry-red bottom grasped in both hands. He was a stripling, ten or eleven, big for his age, and with a good head of meanness already taking over.

"My husband will—" Mrs. Means started, then stopped when Cardigan shook his finger at her.

"Now you shut your big mouth," he said softly. "Is that your brat? That's the meanest kid I've ever seen. He hauled off and hit that little girl over there."

"Why, that's May, his sister! He's got a right . . ."

"Lady, I told you to shut up," Cardigan said. "You can get your bottom paddled as well as that kid's. Now take that tribe and clear out of here. I didn't like your husband and my opinion of the rest of you ain't improved none."

Two of the women helped Mrs. Means to her feet and she said, "What a shame, exposin' the boy's privates that way! My husband will take a horse whip to you."

"If he comes over here," Cardigan said, "he'll go home with one end of the whip wrapped around his neck and the handle shoved—" He stopped suddenly and stood there, anger and embarrassment on his face.

"You'd better go," Lila said.

"With pleasure," Mrs. Denny said. "You're terrible people."

Mrs. Means helped Edgar pull up his trousers and brushed away his tears and got her hand slapped for her trouble. She backhanded him across the mouth and shook him, then they marched out of the yard.

Jim Cardigan said, "I sure put my foot in it then, didn't I? Me and this damned temper. I never do anythin' until I get mad and then it's the wrong thing, or the wrong time."

She studied him a moment, then said, "Jim, for the first time I think I like you. Come in for coffee." She took his arm. "Come on."

He walked with her to the cabin. "I didn't intend to lick that kid, but he hit the girl; there wasn't any call for that. Then I told him to cut it out and he called me a name." He looked at the rough palm of his hand; it was a bright pink. "I guess I really laid it on."

"Some people need it laid on," Lila said. "Jim, you weren't the only one who lost your temper." He looked at her, surprised. "I'd just finished telling them off, telling them to get out and stay out."

"Well, I'll be damned," he said and a smile broke the rough planes of his face. "Ain't that somethin'?" He was still smiling when he lifted his coffee cup and saluted her with it.

Smoke Purcell put up at the hotel as soon as he reached town, stowed his saddlebags, locked his door, and went down to the main street. The north side of town was crowded against a hillside, the houses rising in tiers. All the business houses fronted on the long main street, which was wide and deeply rutted. He walked up one side and down the other and found the government land office wedged in between a saddle shop and a drugstore.

Purcell went inside and stepped up to the counter. The walls were covered with maps and narrow alcoves stored with leather-bound record books and the air was musty, a blend of leather and paper and ink and accumulated dust.

The clerk said, "Thinking of homesteading, friend?"

"I'd like to investigate the grazin' rights on some government land," Purcell said, looking at a large wall map. He put his finger on the area. "Right here."

"That country's being grazed now," the clerk said.

Purcell looked at him. "Who has the rights?"

"Well, no one," the clerk said. "It's grazed by common usage."

"I know about that," Purcell said. "The cattlemen used open range for years until someone thought to file for grazin' rights." He tapped the spot with his finger. "I want to file on that."

The clerk shrugged. "You understand about mineral rights and . . ."

"And timber rights," Purcell finished. "I want only grazing privileges. What's the acreage of that parcel?" He traced a boundary with his finger.

Checking carefully, the clerk said, "Six sections.

That'd come to nearly three hundred dollars a quarter, the first quarter paid in advance."

"Let's fill out the papers."

"I'm talking cash," the clerk said.

"Hell, so am I," Purcell said. He reached under his coat and shirt and took out his leather money pouch and counted out the three hundred dollars.

The clerk sighed and started preparing the lease. "Seems like a mean trick to play on Means and Denny and the others," he said.

"What's mean about it?" Purcell asked. "They could have taken a lease on grazing rights, couldn't they?"

"Yep," the clerk said. "I guess they didn't want to part with the cash." He looked up. "How long you want this lease to run?"

"Ninety-nine years," Purcell said. "And there's an option to buy or prove-up clause there. I don't want it crossed out either."

The clerk looked at him carefully. "You know about these things, don't you?"

"I know how much trouble cattlemen have, friend. I don't intend to have that kind of trouble. If there comes a time I want to own it, I can prove it up a section at a time." The clerk opened his mouth and Purcell held up his hand. "I know, I can only prove up on one section, but I can also buy the land off anyone else who proves up on it. And havin' grazin' rights gives me the say-so over who homesteads it. Ain't that right now, friend?"

"You're a well-informed man," the clerk said and finished the paperwork. It took some time, and there were several copies to be signed, but an hour later Purcell walked out with the lease in his pocket.

He found the sheriff's office in the basement of the stone courthouse, and paused before a door marked: Val Sansing, Sheriff. Then he knocked, heard a man say something, and walked in. Sansing was at a filing cabinet, putting away "Wanted" posters, and he looked at Purcell with the flat, searching glance lawmen develop.

"Something I can do for you?" Sansing was thirty-some, rather tall and very soft-spoken.

"Purcell's the name. How much does it cost to have a notice posted?"

"Two dollars," Sansing said. "That pays for the filing. A dollar a notice for everyone served. Sit down."

"Thanks," Purcell said. He took a chair by the desk and crossed his legs.

"I've never seen you before."

"First time in town," Purcell said. "I can give you a legal description of the property." He took the lease from his pocket and handed it over and Sansing's expression changed while he read; a furrow formed between his eyes and deep wrinkles appeared on his forehead.

"This land is being grazed now," he said. "Ramey uses it and . . ."

"Ramey's dead," Purcell said, and told him about the fire.

When he was through, Sansing shook his head. "Too bad. It really is. He was getting over his head, you know. Owes money in town. Two or three hundred dollars anyway." He took out a cigar and bit off the end, then scratched a match on the underside of his desk. "Likely I'll have to foreclose and sell the place off to pay the creditors."

"Not if you tell me who they are so I can pay them off four bits on the dollar," Purcell said.

"How do you know they'd accept that?" Sansing asked.

"Because it's a long wait until the court gets through with it. And maybe a longer wait until a buyer comes up with cash." He folded his hands. "I'm trying to make it easier on everyone, Sheriff."

"First you take out grazing rights," Sansing said softly, "knowing full well that you're pushing Means and the others to the wall. Now you want to clear off the debts Ramey left behind. Now, you're either a generous cuss or you're working something up the sleeve I can't see."

"It's an investment," Purcell said. "What's wrong with that?"

"What does Lila say about it?"

"What can she say? Does she want to lose the place?" He shook his head. "Sheriff, I didn't come here to debate the thing. I came to get legal notice filed that the land I just leased is for my use. Now you've got to serve the notices. Right?"

"That's right."

"And if Denny or the others make trouble, you've got to step in and stop it, right?"

"Right again."

"So suppose I pay you now and you tend to servin' the notices." Purcell smiled pleasantly. "I ain't no monster. That land could have been leased by anyone, but no one wanted to do it. Well, I just done it, paid for it with cold cash." He leaned back and crossed his arms. "Now, somebody's goin' to have to pay off Ramey's debts, ain't they? One way or another they've got to be paid. It would be a shame to have a sheriff's sale just for three hundred dollars, wouldn't it?"

"Yes, it would," Sansing said. "But I don't put you in this picture, Purcell."

"Don't try," Purcell said gently. "Now let's get those notices filed." He leaned forward and put his elbow on Sansing's desk. "And when we're through, you might tell me who Ramey owed. I could find out eventually myself, couldn't I?"

CHAPTER 6

After going to the store and three other places, Smoke Purcell stopped to consider just how well he was doing. He'd paid off one bill of over a hundred dollars for less than half that amount, and he'd settled the other two accounts for even less. Now he had one more, a tough one. He walked down the street to the saloon and pushed open the door.

The drinking and talking went on in the front but he had no interest in it, other than to stop at the bar to ask a question. Then he walked on back, opened a door and closed it, blocking out the babble and clink of glasses. Green-topped poker tables were evenly spaced around the four walls, and the house man was conducting a listless game of blackjack. Purcell walked over and stood nearby.

He watched the game for a moment, then the gambler spoke without looking up. "You're bothering me, friend."

"I want to talk to you," Purcell said.

The three men at the table looked at him but the gambler kept his attention on his cards. A woman opened the door from the saloon and came back with a full stein of beer and placed it by the gambler's left elbow. She was a fair, shapely woman in her early twenties and Purcell gave her a long glance, then looked back at the gambler.

"My pappy used to tell me never to mix talk and play," the gambler said.

"Did your pappy have anything funny to say about money?"

"For a fact, he didn't," the gambler said and looked up. His face was thin, he was clean-shaven and his eyes were a deep blue; frank, friendly eyes that Purcell thought incongruous in a gambling man. "What's on your mind?"

"Paul Ramey owed you money."

"Everybody in town knows that."

"How much did he owe?" Purcell asked.

The gambler frowned. "That's Ramey's business."

"Ramey's dead. You tell me if you want to get paid."

After thinking about that for a moment, the gambler said, "Two hundred dollars. He was a terrible poker player."

"Maybe you're too good a poker player," Purcell said. He reached out and touched one man on the shoulder and gently nudged and as the man got up quickly, Purcell sat down across from the gambler. "I'll tell you what I'll do. I'll play you one hand of five-card draw, no-hole card, double or nothing."

"Who could turn down a thing like that?" the gambler said. He picked up the deck and shuffled rapidly and when he offered the cut to

Purcell, Smoke shook his head and nodded to the woman.

"Let her do it."

She made the cut and the gambler dealt Purcell a queen of hearts. He dealt himself an ace, and gave Purcell a nine of diamonds, and himself a six of clubs. Purcell got a ten of spades, and the gambler took an ace, then he gave Purcell another queen. The next card was the gambler's and it was a deuce of clubs, then he flipped over Purcell's last card, a third queen.

"Hold it a minute," Purcell said, getting up. "I'll be back."

He stepped quickly out of the room and over to the back of the bar. The bartender was at the far end and before he could stop Purcell, the sawed-off shotgun had been lifted.

"What are you doin' with that?" the bartender asked. "You put that back."

"You'll get it back," Purcell said and took it into the back room. He straddled his chair and laid the shotgun on the table, the muzzle pointing at the gambler, and said, "Now turn your card up and if it's an ace I'll blow you into the next county."

The gambler sat with his hands flat on the table, no expression at all in his eyes.

Purcell said, "Well? What's it goin' to be?" Then he looked at the woman. "Turn his card up."

"Wait!" the gambler said. "I don't know what that card is. But suppose it is the ace?"

"There will be a loud boom," Purcell said.

The door behind was opened and men crowded there to see what was going on, but they made no sound, as though they were afraid to upset some delicate balance.

"Ramey's dead," the gambler said. "He doesn't owe me anything."

"I didn't think he did," Purcell said matter-of-factly. He nodded toward the card. "Want to take a chance?" When the gambler hesitated, Purcell reached out and flipped it over, a five of diamonds.

The gambler let the breath run out of him in a long sigh, and Purcell got up, saying, "Been nice playing with you, friend."

At the door he handed the shotgun to the bartender and walked out and across the street. He went into the hotel and up the stairs to his room and put a match to the lamp, then sat down on the bed, feeling the full weight of weariness that too little sleep had brought.

He tugged off his boots and took off his shirt and washed his hands and face, then turned his head quickly when a soft knock rattled his door. Before opening it, he went to his saddlebag and took out his pistol, swinging out the cylinder to see that all six holes were filled, then he snapped it closed and went to the door and opened it.

The woman who had brought the gambler his beer stepped in and Purcell closed the door. She said, "Do you know what you did tonight?"

"I wiped out a man's debt."

"Is that all?" She took off her coat and dropped it on the bed. "Pete Manning is a nice fella. He doesn't scare easily."

"He did tonight," Purcell said. "Are you his woman?"

She shook her head. "I like him. So do a lot of people. And I don't like you."

"Did you come here to tell me that?"

"That's right."

Purcell laughed and reached for her before she knew what he was doing. He twisted one arm behind her and brought her against him hard enough to make her gasp, then he held her to him while he kissed her, not gently, but with a full, frightening hunger. She struggled until she was convinced it was useless then let him have his way. Finally he let her go.

As soon as she was free, she hauled back a hand to slap him but he caught her wrist, putting on pressure that made her cry out and drop to her knees. Purcell said, "Don't try that with me, honey."

He turned loose his grip and she knelt on the floor, rubbing her wrist and crying. He walked over to the dressing table and put his pistol in a drawer. Then he turned and leaned his buttocks against it and looked at her.

"Cry all night and it won't do you any good," he said.

She wiped her eyes and looked at him. "You hurt me."

"Is that the first hurt you've ever had?" he asked. "What's your name?"

"Helen. Helen Jensen."

"You want to stay the night?" Purcell asked.

She gasped and got to her feet, her face flushed with anger.

He laughed and said, "I believe in asking right out."

"What kind of a man are you?" she asked.

He shrugged. "What kind do you want me to be? A man is a lot of things to a lot of people, you know. It's the ones who can't adapt who have all the trouble." He took out his tobacco and rolled a cigarette. "Now let's look at this with a little common sense, shall we? You're in a saloon. Came in for a drink? Naw, I don't think so. So what's the answer? Tryin' to make a buck or two?"

"You swine, I own the place," she said. "My father left it to me."

"Well, I've got nothin' against a woman with money," Purcell said. "You can still stay the night if you want."

She wanted to say something, to swear, or to throw something, but she was too angry for any of that. Instead she clenched her fists, then turned to the door and slammed out.

He finished his cigarette and snuffed it out and sat down on the bed when another knock disturbed him. "Come in," he said and was surprised when Val Sansing stepped into the room.

Sansing closed the door and leaned against it. "I heard about that business with Pete Manning."

"It was never meant to be a secret," Purcell said. "If a man hasn't got the guts, then he shouldn't gamble."

"Manning is one of the few honest gamblers I know," Sansing said. "Maybe that's why he doesn't always have a big roll in his poke. Pete's a good judge of people and trusts a lot to luck."

"He didn't think much of it tonight," Purcell commented. "You want to sit down and relax or do you want to stand there like you're expecting me to draw on you?" He took his hands from behind his head. "See, no gun." He lifted the pillow and Sansing stiffened. Purcell laughed. "None there either. Why don't you sit down? I hate to see a man all tensed up."

Sansing came over to the chair. "You like to push a man, don't you?"

"Was I doin' that? I'm sure sorry. Didn't mean to."

"I saw Helen Jensen in the lobby," Sansing said. "I wouldn't want to see her hurt by anyone. You get what I mean?"

"Sheriff, it seems like you're set on taking care of everybody in the whole county," Purcell said. "That must keep you pretty busy."

Sansing sighed and got up. "Purcell, you ought to

67

worry more about yourself. You keep on this way and you won't have a friend left."

"I'll always have one," Purcell said. "And how many does a man really need?"

"All right," Sansing said and went out. Purcell waited until he heard the footsteps fade, then got up, bolted his door and went back to the bed to sleep.

It came to him almost immediately.

Val Sansing had some notices to post, and he left town early in the morning and took the valley road, stopping at Joe Harms's place first. Denny and his oldest boy were there, which suited Sansing for it saved him a three-mile ride.

They came from the house as he dismounted by the barn and Harms shook hands. "Don't see much of you out this way, Sheriff," he said, then laughed. "Of course, we don't break many laws."

"Part of my job is trying to keep folks from breakin' 'em as well as catchin' 'em afterward," Sansing said. He unbuttoned his coat and brought out his sheaf of notices and handed one to each man. "That government land's been filed on for grazing rights. You'll have to move your sheep off it, and stay off. The law gives you thirty days."

They seemed too stunned to speak; they looked at each other and at Val Sansing. Then Denny said, "They can't do that!"

"It's already been done," Sansing said. "Frankly, you've had all these years to file yourselves. I can't see why you're so surprised. Didn't you think anyone would ever file on that land?"

"Who the hell around here had the money?" Harms said. He blew out a long breath. "By God, law or no law, I'm not movin' my sheep until spring. Where the hell can I get graze with two feet of snow on the ground? Now I ask you."

"Joe, there's no sense lettin' your mad cloud your thinkin'," Sansing said. "If you don't move your sheep, they can be moved for you and you'd have to pay to have it done. If you didn't have the money, an attachment could be put on the sheep and they'd be sold to satisfy the bill."

Mort Denny said, "You ain't told us who took out the lease."

"Purcell, the new man at the Ramey place."

"Knew it," Denny said. "Just knew it! Where'd he get the money? Sheriff, you ought to investigate that fella. I'll bet he's wanted for robbery or somethin'."

"I intend to," Sansing said. "But that doesn't change anything. The law's the law and you'll have to comply with it." He turned to his horse and mounted up. "Sorry. But you know that."

He rode out to make other calls and Denny went back into the house, Harms and Denny's boy following. They poured some coffee and took it to the parlor, and when Denny's wife poked her head in and said, "What'd he want?" Denny glowered at her and she retreated to the kitchen.

Finally Harms said, "It's a shame that Ray Kline wasn't a better shot."

"That's a fact," Denny said. "What are we goin' to do?"

"I ain't thought it out yet," Harms said.

Asa Denny swallowed and said, "Pa, I . . ."

"Shut your mouth now, son," Denny said. "You don't want to be a blabbermouth. Let your old pa do the thinkin'; them that does the thinkin' has the right to the talkin'. I've told you that a hundred times."

"Why don't you let the boy have his say, Mort?"

"All right," Denny said flatly. "Some people just have to be shown everything." He looked at Asa. "Go ahead, son, say your mind. Mr. Harms wants to hear what you have to say."

The boy swallowed again. "Well, I just thought we ought to go talk to this Purcell again, Pa. No harm can come of it."

Mort Denny laughed and slapped his leg, then sobered quickly. "That's a thought? You made that up all by yourself in your own head? Boy, it's plain that you can't think and that you have no pride. Me go to him and beg?" He laughed without humor. "I'd as soon make a pact with Lucifer. Yes, sir, I believe I would."

"Now wait a minute," Harms said. "I'd go talk to Purcell. Hell, yes, if it would save me trouble."

"He'd mock you," Denny said. "Will you never learn that you can't do business with people who aren't Christians? There's only one thing a man like Purcell understands, and that's force. If we band together, go to him then, well-armed, with right and God on our side, he'll back up quick enough. I know his kind."

"I don't know his kind," Harms said. "But I never knew a man, unless he was dead drunk, that you couldn't talk some sense to. I'm goin' and I'll join any other man who wants to come with me. And I ain't takin' a gun because I'm no shot at all and don't want my head blown off because he don't know it."

"It's a fool's errand," Denny said, "but I've never let a friend down. When do you want to go?"

"As soon as I can get my coat on," Harms said.

CHAPTER 7

Jim Cardigan was working near the foundation of the barn when Smoke Purcell returned, and he stuck the shovel into the ground and walked over while Purcell dismounted.

"You took your time," Cardigan said.

Purcell laughed and shifted a package from one arm to the other and reached inside his coat and handed Cardigan a bottle of whiskey. "The best in town," he said. "From me to you." Then he turned his head as Lila opened the door; he slapped Cardigan on the arm and started to turn, but Cardigan held him.

"What's in the package?"

"A little present for the lady," Purcell said. He smiled at Lila and handed her the package. "Somethin' I thought you'd like. Go try it on."

"What? Why, Smoke, I never expected . . ."

"Of course you didn't," he said, patting her arm. "Go on now. Surprise me."

She was excited about it, Cardigan could see, as though she had never been given many presents; she laughed and turned and ran back to the cabin.

Cardigan said, "What the hell went on in town?"

"I've got a job for you," Purcell said, evading the question.

"Ain't you always?"

"I want you to hitch up the wagon and go in and lay in some supplies. If you get goin' now, you can make it back in the mornin'." The smooth youthfulness of his face broke into a toothy smile. "Jim, you need some town livin'. I can always tell, you know. You get a little grim around the mouth." His manner changed and his voice turned softly confidential. "Look, Jim, I want to make a little private time here. All right? We need supplies; I don't want to be runnin' back and forth all the time. And I'd like to be alone with Lila, for some friendly kind of talk. All right? She don't know I squared off her brother's debts and took out that grazing lease. These things always surprise a woman."

"They kinda surprise me too," said Cardigan.

Purcell was still smiling. "I need to be alone with her to tell her in my own way, the right way." He slapped Cardigan on the shoulder. "So how about hitching up and getting out of here?"

"The wagon's kind of comin' apart," Cardigan said. "Suppose I ride in and rent a wagon from the livery?"

"You're gettin' the idea," Purcell said. "Take my horse and save some time."

"You're really in a hurry, ain't you?" He walked over and picked up his coat and slipped into it. "I cleaned up . . ."

"Yeah, I can see that you did," Purcell said and watched Jim Cardigan mount up. He put his hand on Cardigan's knee. "When you're buyin' at the

73

store, remember she's a woman and get somethin' besides backfat and beans."

"Sure, Smoke."

"And don't hurry back. Enjoy yourself."

"I won't get drunk," Cardigan said and rode out.

Purcell watched him go, then he rolled a cigarette and walked to the cabin. At the door he paused a moment, then walked in and went over to the kitchen stove and poured a cup of coffee. While he stood there, Lila came out of the bedroom and stopped in the doorway.

Smoke Purcell smiled and said, "Somehow I knew you'd fill out that dress when I saw it in the store."

"It—it's beautiful," Lila said. "I've never worn anything like it before."

He looked at her smooth bare shoulders and breasts tight in the velvet bodice; the full, sweeping skirt touched the floor and whispered when she moved. "I've seen the rich women in Cheyenne wear dresses like that, Lila. They'd go to balls and things in the evenin' dressed like that. I just had to buy it for you."

"Smoke, where would I wear it?" She spread her hands and smiled and shook her head. "It isn't very practical."

"Wear it for me, here, like now," he said. "Ain't that reason enough?" He put down his coffee cup without taking his eyes off her and walked up to her

74

and stood close without touching her and his voice was a soft wind and there was a veiled mystery in his eyes. "I've been a wanderin' man, Lila, but I ain't no more. You know why that is?"

"Smoke, not now," she said.

"I'm goin' to finish," he said. "And I'm not goin' to rush you, Lila, but you've got to hear me out. The first time I looked at you I knew you was the prettiest thing I'd ever seen, and I couldn't leave. No power could make me leave. Maybe you don't like me. Maybe someday you'll say, 'Get out and keep goin',' and I'll . . ."

"Smoke, I wouldn't do that!"

He held up his hand. "I ain't finished yet." His manner saddened and his voice was soft with regret. "You've just lost your brother, all you had in the world, and my heart's just too full to talk about it. I bought you the dress, thinkin' it might cheer you up a little, then when I saw you in it, I knew I bought it because I just can't get you out of my mind at all. I know it's too soon, too short an acquaintance even to say a thing like that, but I wanted to speak. I guess I pretty well have to anyway, otherwise you'd think it kind of strange that I paid off your brother's debts,"—she gave a little gasp, but he hurried on—"and also took out a grazing lease." Lila opened her mouth and he covered it, very gently, with his hand. "I just wanted to let you know that I'll be here as long as you need me and that I'll take care of you, take

75

care of everything for you, and maybe in time, well, you know . . ."

"Smoke," she said and touched him, then she put her arms around him and laid her head against him. "I feel safe now. And I haven't felt this way in a long time." She pulled her head back and looked at him and her hands came to his face and touched his cheeks. "Can I ever explain to you how it's been to be alone? Because that's really the way it has been. But this is all new to me and you'll have to give me time."

"You know I wouldn't push you, Lila."

She nodded. "Yes, you're a good man, Smoke." Her eyes never left his and slowly, gently, she put her lips against his and her arms went about him, tightening, and he kissed her for a long moment before letting her go. When she stepped back, her face was flushed and she put a hand to her cheek. "My," she said, then turned and went into the bedroom and closed the door.

He turned back to his coffee, reheating it by adding to the cup, then went to the window as he heard a noise in the yard. Denny and Harms were walking toward the door. He opened it before they could knock and there they just stood, surprise on their faces.

"Do come in, neighbors," Purcell said, stepping aside. "Get you some coffee, maybe?" He didn't wait for their answer, but fetched two cups and poured. "Sit down. Mighty neighborly for you to call. Lila's in the bedroom. Lila, we got company!"

As she came out, Denny said, "Sheriff Sansing called on us."

"A very efficient man, Sansing," Purcell said. "I guess he posted the notice."

They nodded, and Harms said, "Purcell, we can't get our flocks out of that country in the time he gave us."

"I know that," Purcell said. "And there's no need to." He smiled genuinely. "Neighbors, you go ahead and graze there all you want to. You have my permission and you've got a witness that I said it."

Harms and Denny looked at each other, then Denny said, "A Christian attitude. Indeed it is. But why go to the trouble to spend all that money on a grazin' lease if you're goin' to share it with us?"

"To keep some speculator from doin' it," Purcell said and slapped the table. "The world's full of sly people, neighbor. Yes, sir, men who'll steal your elk's tooth off your watch chain while askin' you for the time. It's the only way to protect what you got. I had the money and I took out the lease. Simple as that. Now if the shoe had been on the other foot, you havin' the money, I'd have asked you to do the same."

Harms laughed. "I told you talkin' it over was the thing to do, Mort. That boy of yours has a head on him."

"Ain't much in it," Denny said.

"Did you come here expectin' trouble?" Purcell

asked in a tone that shamed them for even thinking such a thing. "Why, you've hurt me, neighbors. You really have. I know we didn't get off to much of a start, and that little misunderstandin' we had in the hills didn't help much, but I'm not a man to bear a grudge. No, sir, too many people spend their lives bearin' grudges. That's why we get wrinkled when we get old, holdin' in all that stored-up meanness."

"You're a godly man," Denny said. "They're few these days." He finished his coffee and put the cup aside. "Well, Joe, I guess we'd better get back. Purcell, about Kline—he acted hasty the other night. I'll pray for him if you'll try to forgive him."

"Forgiven," Purcell said, spreading his hands wide. "A clean slate, neighbor. Peace and love."

"Bless you," Denny said. "Let's go, Joe." He smiled at Lila Ramey. "It has been a pleasure, miss."

Purcell let them out and walked a way with them, then went back to the cabin and found Lila in the kitchen. She giggled and said, "You know, I almost came out and asked you to button up the back of my dress; you can imagine how that would have looked to Denny."

She turned around and he saw that the buttons she could not easily reach were still undone. He buttoned them for her, then put his arms around her. "It's good to know you have peace with your neighbors. After the things that happened, I wasn't sure if we'd ever get along. They didn't understand me, I guess." Then he kissed her on the neck. "I've got work to do. It wouldn't do for Jim to get the idea that he's the only one who can get anythin' done."

Jim Cardigan tied up in front of the general store and went inside, carefully stamping snow off his boots first; he even took a broom from a display barrel and cleaned them.

The owner was behind the counter. He had been watching Cardigan and when he came in, offered him a cigar. Cardigan took it, sniffed it, priced it mentally at a nickel, then said, "What's this for?"

"Been in business eighteen years," the man said. "It ain't often that my customers are considerate enough to clean off their boots. In the winter it's water puddles from melted snow. Spring it's mud, and summer and fall it's manure. You've just earned yourself a cigar." He scratched a match and held it while Cardigan bit off the end and drew deeply.

"Mighty good cigar," he said. "I'd like to order if you've got pencil and paper handy."

The storekeeper produced them and laughed. "Without those I'd be broke. What'll it be?"

Jim Cardigan walked around the store and looked at the canned goods and when a thing took his fancy, he ordered it and the storekeeper filled a page and started on another. Then Cardigan found a large copper skillet and it took his fancy as he thought of the black iron one Lila used.

"How much for this?"

The storekeeper shook his head. "Wish I'd never bought that. Too expensive. Made back East, you know. Copper-plated."

"How much?"

"Five dollars, and I should apologize."

"I'll take it," Cardigan said. "And some polish to keep it shiny." He walked back to the counter. "You want to add that up, I'll pay for it. Can I rent a wagon at the stable?"

"An order this big I'll have delivered."

"Then take it to the Ramey place," Cardigan said.

The storekeeper looked up quickly. "You the other one?"

"The other one what?"

"The other tough who has taken over out there?"

Cardigan frowned. "I don't know about bein' tough, or takin' over for that matter. My partner and I are helpin' out, that's all."

"Like payin' off a dead man's debts at the point of a gun?"

"You're one up on me there, friend," Cardigan said. "I don't know anythin' about that."

The storekeeper looked at him for a minute, then said, "Maybe you don't, but I'd keep my mouth shut about bein' that fella's partner. Especially in the saloon."

"You want to explain that?"

"Why not?" He put his hands flat on the counter and looked at Jim Cardigan. He was fifty, maybe a little more, a solid man, who wasn't particularly frightened by the things life bumped him against, and Cardigan put him down as a man who couldn't be pushed. "Your friend paid Paul Ramey's bill; I took forty cents on the dollar and considered myself lucky to get that much. I took the money because I'm in business, but I told your friend that I didn't want any more of his. So he sends you."

"I didn't know this," Cardigan said, simply, quietly, and with such a ring of truth that the storekeeper relaxed and let some of the anger fade from his face. "Smoke does a lot of things I don't know about, I guess."

"Want some applejack? I've got a keg here." He went over to the hardware section and brought back two tin cups and filled them. "Bert Staffen's the name. I didn't get yours." Cardigan told him and they drank the applejack. "Your friend's a cocky fella," Staffen said. "He pushes a man the wrong way. I've never liked it when a man tells me I can take his offer or go to hell. You want some good advice? Split off from Purcell. Don't wait, Cardigan. Do it now."

A frown built on Cardigan's blunt face. "Smoke was little more'n a kid when I first knew him. It was in a north Texas cow camp and they were goin' to make him ride a mean horse just for the fun of it."

"And you stopped it?" Staffen asked.

Cardigan nodded. "We kind of fell in together and drifted to Wyoming." He looked into the tin cup at the last of the applejack, then finished it off and put the cup on the counter. "Before I met Smoke, I used to bust my pay on booze and cards and land in jail to sleep it off. Sometimes an outfit would just pull up and leave me. Smoke's always there if I go on a toot, Staffen. It's good for a man to know there's always someone."

Bert Staffen smiled and shook his head. "Why is it that the good men always make the biggest fools? Have some more applejack."

"That's kind of got a belt to it, ain't it?"

"Good, though," Staffen said and filled the cups.

CHAPTER 8

The barn raising was a big event and a large crowd formed early, the men getting right down to the business of putting up walls, and the women preparing to cook. Smoke Purcell was an excellent supervisor, and he spent the day going about, complimenting his neighbors on their skill with tools, and urging them to greater effort. Cardigan, who worked along with the others, waited to see just how much Purcell would get them to do. By evening a small bunkhouse and tool shed had been built, along with a stout stock pen by the east side of the barn.

It was late by the time the eating and talk was over, and when they finally all got in their bobsleds and on their horses and left, Lila Ramey sagged weakly into a chair in the kitchen. Purcell and Cardigan poured coffee for themselves and Cardigan stood by the stove and smoked a cigarette.

"A man," he said, "couldn't take many days like this." He looked at Smoke Purcell and laughed. "You were a pretty busy fella out there today. I'll bet they never seen a man work so hard."

"You sore because you picked up a callous?" Purcell asked. He looked at Cardigan, the lamplight shining on his smooth, untroubled face. "I wanted more than a barn and I got it. Saves time."

"We runnin' out of that?"

"Spring'll be here before you know it," Purcell said. "Jim, I've been thinkin'. What kind of meat do you usually eat?"

"Beef," Cardigan said without hesitation. "When I order a meal, I order a beef steak. Why?"

"And when you ain't orderin'?" Cardigan rowned and Purcell laughed. "You eat bacon. More bacon than anything else."

Lila rested her head on her folded arms, and she looked up, raising her head a little. "What are you saying, Smoke?"

"That we ought to be raisin' hogs."

"Hogs?" Cardigan shouted. "That's goin' too far!"

"You shut up and listen," Purcell said. "There's good money in hogs, and we need somethin' to pull this place into shape. Not meaning to say anythin' disrespectful against the dead, but this place has gone to pot. Ramey sold off too many head of stock to take the pressure off him. Come spring, we'll be in a fix if we don't make a change. Hogs can be turned into a quick profit, Jim. I've seen it done. Remember that fella in Texas who lost his herd to fever? Before anyone found out he was broke, he bought hogs on credit and . . ."

"Yeah, I remember him," Cardigan said. "But a hog farmer . . ."

"Only for a while," Parcel said. "Only until the rest of the sheep can be sold off and the grass fallows a season. Then it's white-faced cattle, Jim."

"You are finally talkin' a language I can under-stand," Cardigan said.

"Wait a minute," Lila Ramey said. "Smoke, it's all a nice dream but I've heard my brother talk about it until I no longer believe it. It takes land to work cattle, and men, and I don't have either one."

Purcell laughed softly. "You just leave it to me, huh? Jim, I want you to take care of things here while I'm gone. Build a dozen hoghouses but keep them in the barn. I don't want Denny or any of the others finding out . . ."

"Where you goin' now?" Cardigan asked.

"Chicago," Purcell said casually.

They stared at him, then Cardigan laughed. "Smoke, now let's slow down a minute and . . ."

"How much money have you got?" Purcell asked.

Cardigan dug into his pocket and counted it. "About sixty dollars."

Purcell looked at Lila. "And you?"

"A little over a hundred," she said.

"You keep yours," Purcell said. "Give me the money, Jim."

Cardigan handed it over, saying, "Understand, I worked hard for that so watch how you spend it."

"If you watched how you spent it, you'd have more than sixty dollars," Purcell said. "I ought to be back in two weeks, maybe three."

"When," Cardigan asked, "are you going to take this trip?"

"I'll leave tonight," Purcell said matter-of-factly.

Their surprise amused him. "What's the use of waitin'? I'll go into town, get my ticket, and sleep in the depot until train time."

Lila said, "I'm not saying not to go, but explain the difference between going tonight and tomorrow morning."

"It's because tonight he'd be goin'," Cardigan said. "Tomorrow's always a long ways off to Smoke." He kept looking at Purcell, but talking to Lila Ramey. "Did you ever see a dog that just couldn't get settled down? He'll lay one way awhile, then flop over, then get up and turn around, and then move to another spot. Smoke's like that. He has got to prowl, to move. Never knew him to stop."

"Why don't you shut your funny face?" Purcell said. "If you've got somethin' to say, then say it. Just don't run off at the mouth."

Cardigan shrugged. "You'd better get goin' if you're goin'. That train may pull out before you get there."

"Have your joke," Purcell said. "If it wasn't for me, you'd be nothin'."

"I thought," Cardigan said softly, "that I was nothin' in spite of all you've tried to do for me."

"I'm wastin' time," Purcell said and went out to saddle his horse.

Cardigan turned again to the coffeepot and refilled his cup.

"Why do you let him talk to you like that?" Lila Ramey asked him.

"What does it hurt?"

"You," she said.

He looked at her a long moment. "Oh, I guess not. I'll sleep in the barn." He went out, taking the cup of coffee with him.

Purcell had a lantern hung in the barn when Cardigan came in, and he turned his head briefly and looked at him. "What were you trying to do in there?" he asked.

"What do you mean?" Cardigan asked. He threw down his bedroll and opened it.

"You want to play dumb, is that it?" He tightened the cinch. "Don't sit on your backside while I'm gone." He looked at Cardigan, then reached out and slapped across the brim of his hat. "One of these days we'll be rollin' in clover. You wait and see."

"Sure," Cardigan said. "I've got nothin' better to do."

Purcell led his horse out of the barn and closed the door, then went on to the house. Lila was still in the kitchen when he stepped inside and closed the door. She turned her head and looked at him, then said, "Sit down, Smoke. Please. I want to say something."

He shrugged and pulled back a chair, then waited.

"Something's wrong."

"I wouldn't know what," he said, his expression innocent.

"You're doing too much."

"No, not nearly enough," he said. "Lila, one of

these days I want to do some serious talking to you. You understand what I mean? And I don't want to come to you with empty hands. I want you to know then that I'm a doin' man, not just a talkin' man lookin' for a place to stay." He hesitated, as though turning these things over in his mind. "I've got some pretty old-fashioned ideas about what a man should bring to a woman. How can I do these things if I don't get on my pony and just do 'em?" He reached out and took her hands. "A man can catch a glimpse of someone and know right off that, well, there's just no use in lookin' any further. Jim and me, we came here by accident. Jim, he doesn't need much of a reason for doin' the things he does, but I do. I don't stay because I've got a place to sleep and somethin' to eat. And I wouldn't ask any woman to marry me unless I'd showed her that I was someone capable of doin' right by her."

"Is that what you're thinking of, marrying me?"

He nodded. "But it's not time to talk about that yet," he said. "In the spring, maybe, when you know me good." He got up and, bending easily toward her, cupped her face in his hands and kissed her. "I'll be back. You wait."

Then he went out and got on his horse and swung out on the town road. The weather was cold enough to bite through his heavy coat, but he didn't mind that for he was warmed by a good feeling, a feeling he'd always thought about but

88

believed would never come to him. He knew that he was through with riding for another man. Come next winter, he'd be the man to talk to in this lick, the man to deal with, and he didn't care to speculate further than that, for that much satisfied him.

By the time he reached town, the saloon had been closed, although there were still some lamps lighted and the door was open. He went in and found the bartender and Helen Jensen adding up the day's take. Giving him no more than a glance, she said tartly, "At this hour I don't even want to know what you want."

"I'll just back up to the stove and toast a bit," Purcell said.

She looked at him a moment, then went on counting. When it was done, the bartender put on his hat and coat and mittens and went out.

Purcell said, "Ain't you goin' to lock the door?"

"After you leave," Helen Jensen said.

"Now you're not mad at me, are you?"

She shook her head. "I have to like someone to get really mad. Why don't you just leave?"

"I ain't warm yet."

"Go on down to the depot. They always keep the stove going there."

He stepped away from the stove and went to the front door and locked it, then walked around behind the bar. She retreated until she came to the sawed-off shotgun and lifted it, but he ignored her and picked up a bottle and poured himself a drink. She watched him toss it off, then take another. "I like to drink privately," he said. "Join me?"

"I don't use the stuff."

"You're a liar," he said casually. "You like your booze or you'd have sold out when your old man died and invested the money in findin' a husband. You've got your looks, but ready booze will kill those soon enough."

"You're so goddamned smart, ain't you?"

"I kissed you," Purcell said. "It was like sucking a cork."

She stared at him, then tears came to her eyes; she blinked them away. He laughed and said, "When's the train goin' East leave?"

"In the morning. Why?"

"No reason why I shouldn't spend the night here then, is there?"

She stared at him, tears falling openly now down her cheeks. "How could you know? I want you to tell me that. How can you look at me and tell me you know these things?" She put a hand against her breast. "Is there a mark on me? Something you see?" Then she shook her head. "No, it isn't that at all, is it? It's *you*, not me! It's you, with your innocent baby face and rotten heart. People are mirrors of you, aren't they? You see the rottenness because you know what it really is."

"Pretty speech," he said and picked up a full bottle and two glasses. "You want to kill this with me? I get sweet when I've had something to drink."

"Sweet?" She laughed. "You make that into a dirty word."

He shrugged and leaned against the bar. "You ever figure out why you're not married?"

"I don't want to hear your . . ."

"You're goin' to shut your mouth and listen," he said, a dry hardness coming into his voice. "I'll bet you spend a lot of time dreamin' about gettin' a good man and spendin' your life bein' a good woman for him. Honey, you and I both know that's so much wishy-washy. You don't get good men because you just don't attract 'em. You've got no talent for 'em."

"Oh, you're so smart. Got everything figured out, haven't you?"

"Ain't that the best way?" Purcell asked.

"You don't fool me."

"I never tried to," he said. "Did I ever try to?"

Her lips pulled together grimly. "No, damn it."

"So what's all the talk about?" Purcell asked. He took a step toward her, then stood still and watched as she tightened her hand on the shotgun.

"Give me one reason why I shouldn't let go with both barrels and then tell the sheriff you tried to rob me?"

"He wouldn't believe it," Purcell said easily. "First off, the bartender saw me come in. No, the sheriff wouldn't think I was that stupid. Besides, he knows I don't need money." He smiled and said, "Maybe you could tear your dress and figure out a story to go with it." Then he shook his head. "I guess he wouldn't believe that either. So why don't you put up the shotgun and I'll blow out the lamps and we'll go in the back where you live and take the bottle along with us?"

For a moment he couldn't figure out what she was going to do, then her shoulders slumped slightly and she put the shotgun away behind the bar. Purcell turned out the lamps and went into the rear of the building where she kept two rooms.

He took off his coat and hat and put them on a chair, and looked around. The furniture was good, old but solid, probably taken from her father's home after he died. There was a kitchen and living room combined, and through an archway, her bedroom.

Taking a quick look at it, he laughed. "Real nice." Then he came back to the other room and put his arms around her. As she stiffened, he said, "Now you're goin' to be nice, ain't you?"

"I'll kill you in your sleep," she said.

He laughed. "How'd you explain my bein' in your bed? No, there's one thing for sure about us, Helen. We just don't want people to know too much about us. What we are, we like to keep to ourselves, huh?" He slapped her on the flank. "It's kind of late. You think we ought to waste time?"

"Someday . . ."

"That's a long way off," Purcell said. "It's not someday that counts, but right now. And I'm gettin' tired of talkin'. You know what I mean?"

CHAPTER 9

Without the help of Joe Harms and Asa Denny, Cardigan figured that he would have lost twenty per cent of the sheep. The storm had scattered them, driven them to cover, and only after days of searching did they manage to gather the flocks and bring them down to the lower meadows. Cardigan, who had worked cattle all his life and considered it a lonely way to live, realized now that it was not really lonely at all, not compared to the day-by-day living of a sheepman.

Asa Denny shared his camp for a few days, and gradually the boy's trained silence wore away a little and he talked to Cardigan about sheep, which was about all he knew. The Dennys had ranched two places before this one, one in Arizona, another in Texas, and had lost or been run out of both. Raising sheep on the plains or desert was different, and Asa Denny liked the mountains; it gave the sheep cover during the storms and kept them from drifting too far when left unattended.

But sheep, in the mountains or anywhere else, took a lot of time, and a lot of patience, and Cardigan, who was used to riding, couldn't get used to just sitting.

The others—Harms and Mort Denny and Kline—brought wagons with supplies and established their camps in the high meadows, while Asa Denny had his own work to do and left Cardigan alone, so that chiefly to pass the time, Cardigan built a small lean-to, hoping to make his camp a little more comfortable. But the sheep had to keep moving for they cut grass off close with their sharp teeth and two days later he had to move and build another shelter.

He could see the value of a team and a wagon, for these high meadows were big and a man could wear himself out making and breaking camp.

He figured he had been away from the ranch for eight days, give or take one, when he saw a rider making toward him, then recognized Lila Ramey bundled in a man's coat. She came to his camp and swung down and he took the sack of provisions she had tied to the saddle horn.

"We've just got to get the top and sides built on that wagon," she said. "But somehow it just never got done." Then she smiled. "Down to coffee and beans?"

"Ate the beans this morning," Cardigan said. He took her over to the lean-to and the fire and she bent over and sat down on his blankets; it gave him a strange feeling to have a woman do that.

"There's ham and some biscuits and some cold potatoes and . . ."

"Don't spoil it," he said, smiling. "Let me look for myself." He opened the sack and took out some of the canned goods, then got his skillet and heated it. While he cooked, he said, "I guess the storm didn't leave us too bad off, according to Asa Denny. We figure maybe four or five sheep got done in. The dogs kept 'em pretty well bunched and they hunted cover." He sliced potatoes and ham and cooked them together, as though he couldn't bear to wait. "No word from Smoke?"

She shook her head. "I didn't expect any. It has only been nine days." She raised her knees and wrapped her arms around them. "Jim, if you'd been Smoke, you wouldn't have spent the money, would you?"

"No," he said.

"Why?"

"Because any man that spends money expects somethin' for it," he said solemnly. "And in this case, you wouldn't have the likes of me." He turned his head and looked steadily at her. "You want Smoke for a partner?"

"How do you mean that, 'partner'?"

"You know how I mean it. Is he what you want in a man?"

She rested her head on her knees and thought about it, then said, "Maybe I don't know much about men. But I like Smoke. I liked him from the first moment I saw him because he was gentle and the things he said made me feel good and—well, protected. The morning after the fire, he made coffee and brought it to me, and he was thinking about the burying—those are all kind, considerate things, Jim, things a man does because that's the way he is."

"Yeah," Cardigan said and took the skillet off the fire. He didn't bother with his tin plate and he didn't bother to tell her that he'd made the coffee and that he wanted to get the burying done; he supposed he'd never tell her any of these things. It was just Smoke's way, he guessed, to turn things to his advantage. Like that time the boss left the barn door unlocked and his favorite roan got out. In his excitement to get the horse back, he'd offered a month's pay to any man who brought him back. Cardigan and Purcell found the animal and while Purcell sat his horse and watched, Cardigan ran the animal down, put a rope on him, and almost broke his neck doing it. Then Purcell came up, took the horse back to the boss and collected the money, and all the praise.

No, he just wouldn't tell her about any of those things because he liked her and didn't want to hurt her, which seemed strange because he'd never felt that way about any woman before, somehow couldn't bring himself entirely to trust them.

"This is sure good," Cardigan said between bites. "But you made a long ride to bring it to me."

"Jim, can't you get one of the Denny boys to work for you?"

"It has been in my mind," he said. "I ain't even started on those hoghouses yet and I'd have to go in and get the lumber from town."

She got up. "I'll go see Mort Denny."

"Suppose he says no?"

"Then I'll find someone else," she said and stepped into the saddle.

He finished his meal and cleaned the skillet and spent the rest of the afternoon doing nothing. Toward evening Mort Denny and his youngest boy came over with a wagon and dropped off provisions.

"Made the deal with the Ramey woman," Denny said dryly. "A dollar a day."

"That's man's wages," Cardigan said.

"Take it or leave it. That's what I told her."

"It don't seem like we have much choice," Cardigan said.

"Told her that too," Denny said. "Well?"

"She made the deal," Cardigan said and began to gather his gear. He was ready to clear out in twenty minutes and he hurried about it because he wanted to make the Ramey place before dark. When Smoke got back, Cardigan figured to take him to the barn where it was quiet and have a talk about the sheep business; he had already had his fill of it.

The lamps made a beacon down the valley for Cardigan and he put up his horse and threw his blankets and gear down in a corner of the barn and put a match to a lantern and hung it on a nail driven into the wall.

This was, he thought, a poor way to winter out,

97

staying in a barn when he could be in some town where he could get a drink when he wanted it, or a game of cards to pass the time. Smoke was probably in some Chicago hotel, flat on his back, smoking a cigar right now, and the thought of such comfort irritated Jim Cardigan.

The barn door opened and Lila Ramey came in. "I thought I heard your horse," she said. "Jim, come into the house and have some coffee." She sounded irritated and he wondered what he had done to bring that on.

She went out and he waited a moment, then blew out the lantern and walked to the house. The cup of coffee was waiting on the table, and he sat down.

"I do wish you wouldn't do that, Jim," she said.

He looked up, startled, certain that without thinking he had done something unpardonable. He was always doing something, like that time they were at a dance and he came up to Smoke Purcell, who was talking with a really nice girl, and he'd been introduced and in spite of his self-consciousness had managed to talk. Later, though, Purcell had asked him if he remembered what he had said, and Cardigan couldn't. Then Purcell told him that he'd dropped a cuss word and even repeated it. For a long time Cardigan was bothered by that, made to feel small about it; thereafter he kept his mouth shut around a decent woman.

And that was the way he figured it now, sure that he had made another mistake.

Lila said, "You make me feel guilty, sleeping in the barn, and acting like a—well, like a dog that's never allowed in the house."

"I know my place," Cardigan said. "Don't pay any attention to me because I don't guess I'll hang around too long anyway."

She looked at him, surprise in her eyes. "Are you going somewhere?"

"Well, I ain't goin' to stay here," he said. "This ain't my kind of life. Smoke can have it if he wants it. He has got all the ambition."

"Jim, I really don't understand you at all," Lila said.

"Don't try. A waste of time." He sat with his hands cradled around the coffee cup and finally she sat down across from him, a puzzled look on her face.

"Why do you think," she asked, "that you're worthless?"

He sat for a moment, thinking of an answer. "Some men are cut out to be nothing," he said and drank his coffee. Then he said goodnight and went to the barn to bed down for the night.

At dawn he was up, cutting firewood for her, and had saddled up and ridden out before she could fix breakfast. He figured he'd get a meal in town and that way avoid any more of her questions.

99

He remembered seeing a small saw camp near the southwest edge of town and he went there and bought a wagon load of lumber for eight dollars, then went to the store to get nails.

Bert Staffen was putting up stock and he smiled when Cardigan came in. "Thought you'd've been in before this," he said, then looked over his shoulder at the few customers and the clerk behind the grocery counter. "When they leave we'll have another cup of applejack. Great stuff on a nippy day."

"Do you like me?" Cardigan asked frankly.

Staffen looked at him, surprised. "Yes, I like you. That's a funny question to ask a man."

"I've got a funnier one. Why?"

"Why—hell, because you've got a homely, honest face," Staffen said. He took out his hunting-case watch and opened it. "Near eleven o'clock. I could eat early if you're up to it. They serve a good lunch in the saloon, if you like beer with your meals."

"Sure," Cardigan said. "I came in for a keg of nails though."

"Don't waste a trip to town on a keg of nails," Staffen said and got his coat. He spoke briefly to the clerk while Cardigan waited at the door, then they went out together.

In the saloon they made sandwiches and took them to the bar where Staffen ordered, and they stood there, eating and talking. Staffen was saying, "Your partner's been gone some time now. I don't understand his game."

Cardigan shrugged. "Sometimes I don't either but it never makes much difference to him whether I do or not." He looked past Staffen and the storekeeper turned, then laughed.

"Helen, come over here," Staffen called, then took Jim Cardigan by the arm. "Brought you a new customer. Likes cold cuts and beer. Jim, this is Helen Jensen, the owner of this place."

Cardigan bobbed his head and said, "Never knew a woman . . ."

She held up her hands and said, "Does every man have to start out with that remark? Don't you ever think of anything new?"

"No," Cardigan said. "About all I talk about is what I hear. And I didn't mean to offend you."

She smiled. "Now wait a minute, I was joking. You're new, aren't you?"

Jim Cardigan grinned. "Everybody says that to me the first time they . . ."

Helen Jensen put her hands on top of her head. "All right, all right, I take it back." Her laughter was a warm, pleasant sound. "For that I owe you one beer." She caught the bartender's eye and motioned to Cardigan and Bert Staffen. "Two here, Elmo." She stood between them, turned, elbows back on the edge of the bar. "Where did you find this wandering man, Bert?"

"Came into my store," Staffen said seriously. "It

was a cold blustery day and the door flew open, letting in snow and a cruel wind, and this dark stranger with his hat pulled low."

He kept watching Helen Jensen and when her expression broke into laughter, he lost control of his straight face. "All right, no more questions," she said, glancing at Cardigan. "But I want to tell you something when you trade with this fella. Look on the counter and see if there isn't a small shaker of nutmeg. He keeps it there so he can charge it along with every item on all the orders. That little shaker of nutmeg, sold five thousand times, represents the profit of Staffen's store." She kept shooting glances at Staffen as she told this. "Also, the only reason no one's ever said anything about this is because he always gives a bag of candy to the kids and being charged for nutmeg you never get sort of balances out the candy you get and never pay for."

"Which makes me a pretty good fella to do business with," Staffen said. He looked around the saloon. "Where's Pete Manning?"

"He quit," Helen Jensen said.

Cardigan asked, "Who's Pete Manning?"

"A gambler that used to work here," Helen said.

Staffen's face took on a serious cast. "It's none of my business, but I always thought you and Pete would someday . . ."

"It didn't work out," she said quickly and he took the hint and didn't push the subject. Then she turned to Cardigan. "In to get drunk? I sell good whiskey and give a place to sleep it off without getting your pockets picked."

He shook his head and smiled. "Just came in for lumber and nails. But I'll keep the offer in mind and when Smoke gets back . . ."

"Smoke Purcell?"

He nodded.

"You're the partner?"

Cardigan nodded again.

"Elmo, did you hear that?"

"I sure did," the bartender said, moving down to where they stood. "Hey, Smoke Purcell's friend, look here."

Cardigan turned his head and caught Elmo's swing flush on the jaw. He whirled and went back and fell in the sawdust and skidded a bit and lay still. Elmo opened his palm and put the roll of dimes on the bar.

"What the hell's the idea of this?" Staffen demanded, outraged.

"He just said a dirty word in my place," Helen Jensen said, turning away. "You know I don't allow that. Now get him out of here so we can get some clean sawdust down."

CHAPTER 10

Elmo came from behind the bar with a pitcher of water and casually dumped it in Jim Cardigan's face; he sputtered and shook his head and opened his eyes and kept them opened while they focused. Elmo stood there, bland indifference on his face and the few customers in the place turned their heads and watched, when Cardigan suddenly jackknifed his legs and shot them straight up like pistons, arching his body high to get power.

He caught the bartender with the soles of his boots, caught him right under the jaw and lifted him clean off the floor, lifted him onto the bar where he slid half the length before tumbling off, bringing down glasses and bottles.

Helen Jensen, who had already gone into the back, suddenly popped out as Cardigan got to his feet and braced himself against the bar until the dizziness left him. Elmo was recovering, getting to his feet, and he picked up a bung starter as Cardigan came around behind the bar to get him. He swung hard, aiming for Cardigan's head. Cardigan ducked and Elmo wiped a shelf clean of fifty dollars' worth of liquor. He didn't get a chance to swing again because Cardigan hit him twice, forcing him against the bar; then he stepped back and let the man fall heavily.

The front door popped open and Val Sansing stepped inside. "That's enough!" he said; he had that sharp edge in his voice that held Cardigan. Sansing came over and looked at Elmo, then he swung his glance to Helen Jensen. "What started this?"

Bert Staffen said, "Elmo did." He took the wrapper from a cigar and bit off the end. "Val, I don't think this needs settling in your office. It started here. Let it end here."

"I was walking along the street and heard the glass break a half a block away," Sansing said. "I don't allow fighting in town."

"The fight's over," Staffen said mildly. "Helen, why don't you take Jim in back and fix that cut on his face?" He looked at her and waited and when she hesitated, he smiled. "Don't you owe him that?"

"All right," she said. "Come on along, mister."

Cardigan looked at Sansing, then at Bert Staffen, then he came from behind the bar and followed her to her quarters in back. "I didn't mean to hurt your bartender, but I didn't start that," he said.

She seemed to have no anger at all now; she motioned for him to sit down and got a pan of water and a cloth and some iodine. "I know you didn't," she said and pulled an ottoman in front of him. "You must think I'm pretty bad."

"I don't know what to think," Cardigan admitted. "Suppose you tell me." He looked at her round, pleasant face and waited for her to look at him with a patience that wouldn't be put aside. She dabbed iodine on the cut, his silence making her nervous. When she was through she started to get up, but he held her by the arm. "Don't you have anythin' to say?"

"I'm very sorry now," Helen said. "Isn't that enough?"

Cardigan shook his head. "I'm the one who got knocked down and got the headache. I mention Smoke's name and all hell breaks loose. I want to know why."

"Because I hate him," she said softly. "And because I'm helpless to do anything to him." She got up and put the pan of water on the sideboard, then came back. "You may be like him for all I know. If you are, I'm sorry for you."

He frowned pleasantly. "Lady, I don't know what you're talkin' about. I've known Smoke for some years now and I'd be right proud to be like him. But it ain't in me, I guess. I go on a toot now and then and I fight and I don't have many savin' ways like he does." He grinned. "And when I see a pretty gal like you I usually make a fool of myself over her."

She studied him carefully, as though she were able, by this examination alone, to find the truth and the lies in him. Then she sighed and said, "No, you're not like him at all."

"That's what I've been tellin' you," Cardigan said. "You must not hear too well."

"I hear fine," Helen Jensen said. She was going to get up again, but Cardigan took her hands and held her still.

"You didn't say why you hated Smoke. Or how come you know him," he said.

"Look at me," she said. "Look hard. What kind of a person am I?"

"You look like a nice enough gal to me. What am I supposed to see?"

"What Smoke Purcell sees," Helen Jensen said.

"Now how'm I gonna know what he sees?" Cardigan said with some irritation. "I just told you I thought you was a nice enough gal. Do I need someone to support that kind of comment?"

"No," she said softly. "You'd better go back to the bar. Bert's probably wondering what happened to you." He got up and she put her hand on his arm. "No hard feelings, Jim. Please?"

He smiled. "I'll come in again. Get to know you better."

"I'd like that," she said and he went out and found Staffen glancing at his watch.

"Did you kiss and make up?" Staffen asked.

"No kiss," Cardigan said, "but a man couldn't hardly keep from thinkin' about it, could he?"

He went back to the store with Staffen, got his nails, loaded them on the rented wagon piled high with lumber, then started back to the Ramey place, his saddle horse tied on behind.

There was some daylight left when he got there

and he unloaded the wagon and stacked the wood in the barn, then washed up as Lila called from the house for him to come to supper.

He felt a bit self-conscious at her table; she saw the bruised cut but said nothing about it, which bothered him. Finally he said, "I had a misunderstandin' with a fella."

"That doesn't tell me much," Lila said. He looked at her closely and decided that she was put out with him for being so closemouthed. "I was in the saloon havin' a beer," he said. "That's when it happened."

"Can't you go into town without stopping in the saloon?" she asked. "I've lived with that long enough to be tired of it."

He frowned. "Bert Staffen and I went there for somethin' to eat and we had some beer. Now there's nothin' wrong with that."

She put down her knife and fork. "Now don't use that tone with me, Jim Cardigan!" Then she put her fist to her mouth and turned her head partly away from him, as though she were on the edge of tears and couldn't bear to have him see that.

"I told you I belonged in the barn," he said and started to get up.

But her hand darted out and touched his. "No. Sit down, Jim. Eat your supper. I didn't mean to snap at you."

"Go ahead, if it makes you feel better about somethin'," he said.

"I wish Smoke would get back."

He went on eating and she looked at him, as though he were supposed to express some opinion. Finally he said, "When he does come, I'm leavin'. He don't need me and I ain't so sure I need him."

"Why, where will you go?"

He shrugged. "I don't think it should be your business, or his. Smoke and I ain't signed any agreement to stick together. It has just been convenient, that's all."

"And now it's not?" Lila asked. "Jim, has anything happened to make you feel this way?"

"No," he said, "but I am kind of tired bein' wrong all the time."

"Most of the time I don't understand the things you say, Jim."

He put his knife and fork aside. "Maybe I can explain it, and maybe I can't, but I'll try. Now you take me. Most everyone that knows me will say I ain't worth much, but they all like me. But Smoke, he's not that way. The people that know him say that someday he'll amount to somethin', but they sure don't all agree on likin' him. Now I've made no headway at all in figurin' this out and I don't say it's worth the trouble, but it seems that I've kind of been sawed this way and that over a period of time by how people feel about Smoke." He stopped talking to sort out his thoughts.

"Take you, for instance," he went on. "You're all alone here now, place all run down, ready to go busted. If it was me alone, I'd be content to work my fool head off for you, sleep in the barn, and eat your table scraps as long as you'd have me around. A man like me knows what his chances of gettin' a good woman is, and unless he just wants to go all the way alone, he has got to come to terms with himself. You know me five minutes and I guess anyone with a lick of sense would know that whiskey and cards took my money and what little looks I ever had I lost in fist fights and what not. There's some men, like Smoke, who can look at a woman and smile and get a kiss for it. I'd have to cut a rick of wood and save 'em from a runaway horse before I'd rate the same thing." He spread his hands and smiled. "I guess I'm tired bein' compared with Smoke Purcell. I don't like it none to sit across from a woman and have her resent me because I ain't the man she yearns for." He got up. "I thank you for the supper, but I don't think I'd better come to the house again."

She looked steadily at him. "Jim, are you in love with me?"

"You tell me what love is," he challenged. "What I've got's a real good feelin' and you can call it anything you want." He opened the door and stepped out into the cold night and stood there for a moment before going on to the barn.

He worked nearly ten days on the hoghouses, doing everything inside the barn because he didn't want the neighbors to get wind of it. Personally

110

he didn't care, but he knew Smoke wanted it kept quiet and there was no sense getting him riled by going against him. He was always touchiest when he couldn't have his way.

Purcell came back along toward evening. He had packages under his arms and a new suit on and a derby hat and when he shook hands with Jim Cardigan, Jim could smell the spicy sweetness of whiskey killers on his breath. His eyes were a bit bloodshot but Purcell shrugged mention of this aside, saying that he hadn't slept much on the train.

He went into the house, his arm around Lila Ramey, and Jim Cardigan watched them go, then went into the barn and gathered his things and saddled his horse. He was just about finished when Smoke Purcell came in, saw what he was doing, and laughed.

"You're not serious," Purcell said, smiling.

"It looks like I'm jokin'?" Cardigan said.

"Well, I'm asking you not to do this," Purcell said.

"Go ahead and ask. I'm doin' it. Did you think we'd go on forever, the two of us?"

"Jim, I need you."

"I don't think so," Cardigan said. He started to mount, then turned back. "What's between you and the Jensen woman, Smoke?"

Purcell's smile faded. "Nothin' to concern you."

"All right. But you've got a woman here. Try and remember that."

"Jim, I run my own affairs and I've never asked you for help," Purcell said. "Don't stick your nose in now."

"There's a part of you I don't know," Cardigan said. "That's the part I'm leavin', Smoke." He put his foot in the stirrup and got set to swing up.

"You leave when I tell you," Purcell said and grabbed him, tearing him away from the horse. The sudden movement made the animal shy away; the barn was crowded with new hoghouses and the horse backed into one and reared.

Cardigan's temper swelled and he hit Purcell, a driving punch that shocked him and made him back-step to keep his balance.

"You've bought real trouble now," Purcell said and moved in. He swung but didn't land a solid blow, while Cardigan kept smothering him with his arms and bulky coat, which infuriated Purcell because he always knew he could beat this man and now it just wasn't happening that way.

They grappled and wrestled and the horse snorted and kept backing into the hoghouses until Cardigan butted Purcell in the nose with his head and broke the young man's grip. He hit Purcell again, on the cheekbone, bumping his head aside and making his hat fly off.

Purcell's nose was bleeding and there was an angry welt on his cheekbone and he hadn't even marked Cardigan which fired a blind rage within him, made him wild and careless and wide open to a cool man who fought because he wanted to.

The horse rearing and the sound of the fight itself must have carried to the house for Cardigan heard the door slam, and he knew that Lila was coming to the barn, but he couldn't care about that. He wanted to put Purcell down and he went at it with a serious intent, banging him alongside the jaw, gagging him with a rocky fist in the stomach, and when Purcell bent over, finishing it with a down-smashing blow.

Lila opened the barn door just as Purcell fell and she started toward him, but stopped when Cardigan snapped, "I'm not finished yet!"

He walked over and kicked the roof off one of the hoghouses, then dragged Purcell there and hefted him into it, jackknifed so that his head and feet stuck up over the sides.

"That's a good place for him," Cardigan said.

Lila Ramey stood there with both hands pressed against her mouth. "Why?" she asked. "What made you do this?"

"Ask him."

"Can—can I go to him?" she wanted to know.

"He's yours," Cardigan said. "And good luck with him."

"You hate him," she said softly. "Why?"

"To know him is to hate him," Cardigan said. "And I'm just gettin' to know him. Stupid, ain't I?"

He caught up the reins of his skittery horse and mounted and rode out of the barn, not looking back until he was well clear of the yard, when he stopped and saw her helping him toward the house; even at this distance he could hear Purcell swearing and he knew it was at her because he hated to be weak or to have anyone think he even had a weakness.

"I hope she understands him," he said softly, then patted the horse and started for town. There wasn't much doubt in his mind what he'd do when he got there for he always did the same thing when he had nothing to occupy him but time and loose ends.

CHAPTER 11

Like most men who drink too much when they get started, Jim Cardigan forgot to take a room at the hotel or stable his horse and by closing time, he was in the sawdust on the floor, passed out, and Helen Jensen had the bartender carry him into the back and put him on her bed. Then she sent the bartender out to take Cardigan's horse to the stable.

When he came back, he locked the doors, tallied the cash, and when she didn't come to check it with him, he went to her quarters and knocked. But the door was open so he stepped in. She had stripped Cardigan of coat and boots and had covered him with a blanket.

The bartender said, "Elmo would have thrown the bum out." He looked more carefully at Jim Cardigan. "Say, ain't he the one who put Elmo down?" He lifted his glance to Helen Jensen. "How come you're . . ."

"Why don't you mind your own damned business, Larry?"

"Maybe I'd better. You want to check the money so I can leave?"

"I'll do it tomorrow," she said. "Let yourself out the back. I'll lock the door later."

"Goodnight," the bartender said and left. She listened for the back door closing, then pulled a chair around and sat near the bed, looking at Jim Cardigan.

Most of her life she had been around saloons for her father had always made that his business, and she could not begin to guess the number of men she had seen drunk, or getting drunk, or wishing they could. From the time Cardigan came in to the time he stepped away from the bar and fell, she had watched him. He had spoken to no one except to order his drinks, and had wasted no time with them, tossing them down as though hurrying along a road that had no discernible ending.

He was, she saw, a man rushing along, with a hurt in him, and a regret that had to be blotted out to be tolerated. And when he fell she knew that she'd take care of him, because he needed help, and because he had looked at her without an indecency in his eyes.

When the room grew cold she got up and stoked the fire in the potbellied stove, and afterward got a blanket to cover herself and slept in the chair.

Something woke her, she could not tell what. The room was taking on a chill and the fire was down and she got up to build it again. Then she heard a step in the hall and quickly went to her dresser and got her pistol, but before she could turn, a man said, "You won't need that, Helen."

Pete Manning stood just inside the door, another man with him, a man content to stand back in the shadows. Manning stepped inside and the light then fell more strongly on the other man. He was slight, pinched in the face with a long, thin nose and no expression at all in his eyes.

Helen Jensen said, "Who's he?"

"His name's Rand," Manning said. He took off his coat and gloves; his hands were pink and smooth and very slender.

"Is that all there is to his name?" Helen asked.

"That's enough," Manning said. "I met him in Cheyenne while I was dealing there." He smiled. "Rand's going to work for me. I want to open my table again."

"Well, I don't know about that," Helen said.

"I've already made up my mind," Manning said. He looked at Cardigan. "Have you gone through his pockets yet?" Then he laughed and stepped over to the side of the bed and fisted a handful of Cardigan's shirt and hauled him to a near-sitting position. "You're going downhill, Helen. I thought you could get a better looking man than that."

"Get out of my room, Pete."

Manning dropped Cardigan. "See if you can wake him up, Rand."

"You leave him alone!" Helen snapped. She stood there, still carrying the pistol, and when Rand took a step into the room, she cocked it. Manning held up his hand.

"Helen, he could kill you before you could pull that trigger."

"He doesn't want to hang for it," Helen Jensen said. "What's he going to do, Pete, stand behind you while you deal?"

"Something like that. I'll open my game tomorrow night. And it'll stay open until I get Purcell into it."

He turned to the doorway and smiled, then he and Rand walked to the back door and went out and Helen hurried to lock it. She poked the fire and settled in the chair again with the blanket around her, but sleep was impossible now.

Daylight came, gray and overcast, and she made some coffee, then wet a cloth and laid it over Jim Cardigan's face. He groaned and raised his hand, felt the cloth, then wiped it around a few times and took it away.

He looked at her and tried to sit up, then gave a sharp groan and sagged back, his hand on his head.

"About to bust open?" she asked.

He moaned again, and opened his eyes when she came over with some coffee and helped him sit up to drink it. By the time he had downed half the cup, he was feeling a little better.

"How'd I get here?" he asked.

"I had the bartender carry you," she said. "Can you sit up alone?"

"If I don't die," Cardigan said wearily. "You'd think a man would learn, wouldn't you? Every time I get drunk I go through this." She refilled his coffee cup and he sat on the edge of the bed holding it. "I shouldn't be here. Suppose someone finds out I spent the night here?"

"Suppose they do?" she asked. "What are you doing back in town, Jim? I heard that Smoke came in on the early train."

"We've split up," Cardigan said. He shook his head slowly. "I haven't got it figured out yet, but I just knew I had to get out."

"Where are you going now?"

He shook his head. "Got that to figure out. I ain't got enough money to last me the winter now. A job someplace, I guess."

"Get a job here, in town."

"Like to, but I don't think there's much I can do," he said.

She bit her lip a moment, then got her coat out of the closet. "You drink the coffee. Afterward, shave. My father's razor and soap are in the top drawer of the dresser. I'll be back."

She went out before he could say anything, and he just sat there for a time drinking his coffee until he felt well enough to get up and walk around. It was times like this when he envied some men he knew who could drink the well dry and get up the next morning feeling fine. That just wasn't the way it was with him though and he didn't think it ever would be; he supposed it was a blessing for it kept him from drinking too much too often.

He lathered his face and shaved carefully and combed his hair, and was just done with all this when Helen Jensen came back.

"Go see Bert Staffen," she said.

"About work?"

"You go see him," she repeated.

He nodded. "Helen, how can I thank you for this?"

"Why bother?"

"Because you didn't have to do this," he said. "What do you owe me anyway?" He came over to her and put his hands on her shoulders. "What does a man like me say to a good woman?"

"Oh, stop it, Jim! Do you think you're the only man who's stayed the night here?"

"I don't judge you," he said softly. "I see what I see and to hell with the rest."

She looked at him. "Your friend, Smoke Purcell, spent the night here. He drank like a fish and slapped my face and called me a whore before he left."

He watched her eyes, watched for the slightest break, the first indication that she lied, but he could see that she was not lying and it hurt him, not because he had never known these things, but because she had to tell him and hurt herself in doing it.

Finally she could not bear to look at him any longer and pulled away, turning her head. "Get out, Jim. I've been honest with you. Don't ask

120

me why. I guess I just couldn't bear to cheat a man who has been cheated all his life."

"I'll go, but I'll be back," he said.

"There's nothing for you here," she said.

"We'll see," he said and went out.

There were no early customers in Staffen's store when Jim Cardigan went in; Staffen was in his small back-room office and he motioned for Cardigan to join him there.

"I guess you tied one on last night," Staffen said.

"Damned fool thing to do, wasn't it? But I do things like that."

"Things build up until you can't take it no more, huh?"

"Somethin' like that," Cardigan said.

"How clean is this break with Purcell?"

"It's finished," Cardigan said.

Staffen turned around in his chair and looked at Cardigan, tipping his head back to do so. "Jim, I'm going to level with you. I don't like Purcell. I think he's a no-good bastard. Why and how you ever got hooked up with him in the first place remains a mystery to me. But you've got to be through, do you understand? I won't have a man jumping from one side of the fence to the other."

"You offerin' me a job?"

Staffen nodded. "You'll be a jack-of-all trades, Jim, and I'll work you hard for your money, but you'll be able to look any man in the eye and tell him where you got it."

"I've always been able to do that," Cardigan said. "Has Purcell?"

"Far's I know, he has," Cardigan said, then he hesitated; Staffen noticed it.

"What's bothering you, Jim? Catch your partner in a few lies?"

"How'd you know that?" His initial surprise faded and he said, "I've learned a few things about Smoke that I never knew before, and I guess that don't bother me too much. It's just that I've been his friend all these years, and he ain't really been mine."

"This morning early," Staffen said, "I went to the freight office to check on a shipment due to arrive. And talking to the agent, I found out that Purcell had four livestock cars sided for loading next week. That means he's selling off the Ramey girl's sheep."

"Ain't that her business?"

Staffen shook his head. "Anyone around sheep knows that the wool's no good until spring and they're too thin on skimpy winter graze for butchering. Purcell is up to something slick. He didn't go to Cheyenne for nothing."

"He went to Chicago," Cardigan said.

"Jim, don't be a sucker. Ask the station agent. He took the train for Cheyenne and that's that." He took out two cigars and offered one to Jim Cardigan. "I don't trust a liar, Jim. Do you blame me?"

"No."

"Jim, I'm not going to pump you about Purcell, or what he has got up his sleeve. But I think there's going to come a day when someone's going to have to stop him the hard way, and when that day comes, I want you to stand up and be counted."

"I quit him," Cardigan said. "Ain't that enough?"

"It may not be," Staffen said frankly.

"Don't see how I could promise one way or another," Cardigan declared. "Seems like any man who'd switch so easy would be inclined to do it every time the wind changed." He shook his head. "No, I couldn't say I'd go against Smoke. Through with him, yes, but no more."

"All right," Staffen said, getting up. "I'll show you what to do around here. Fifteen a week and lunch?"

"I've never made more than forty a month in my life," Cardigan said.

A store, Cardigan discovered, was a complex business. Freight was always arriving, goods always had to be put away on the shelves, and the weighing and sacking and cleaning and delivering never ended. The job was not easy work, and for a man who had spent his life on horseback and enjoyed a slightly superior feeling because of it, working on his two legs was something of a humiliation.

He was surprised to find that no one in town felt that such work was unmanly and in the few days he delivered boxes and worked in the store he met a lot of people and wondered why any man would want to spend a lonely life with cattle when he could enjoy the comforts of a town, a steady job, and friends.

Payday came on Saturday night, and after the store closed at ten o'clock and the cleaning up was through, he went to the saloon with Bert Staffen and they had a glass of beer and stood at the bar while the crowd milled about and babbled talk packed the place like loose cotton.

When Staffen had his fill of this, he touched Cardigan on the arm and they went into the poker room where Pete Manning sat at his table, celluloid eyeshade pulled low, and black sleeve protectors shining.

Rand stood back, directly behind Manning, a thin shadow with a pearl-handled pistol tied to his leg. The cluster of shaded lamps threw light down on the poker table and when Staffen and Cardigan came into the room, the whites of Rand's eyes shifted as he looked them over.

"King bets," Manning said. He put out the cards, then looked up at Jim Cardigan. "Where's your friend?"

"How do I know?"

"I want to play with him. Tell him that."

"Tell him yourself," Cardigan said.

"Maybe you'd like to sit in?" Manning invited.

"Thanks, no," Cardigan told him.

Manning smiled. "Afraid of losing your money?"

"No," Cardigan said pleasantly. "I'm afraid you might get your smart mouth going and then I'd have to shut it for you." He looked at Rand. "And because you've got that trained ape, I'd have to take that gun away from him and spank his little hands. And that's too much exercise for a working man."

Color left Pete Manning's face and he sat motionless for a moment, looking at Jim Cardigan, who stared back. Then Manning said, "Your turn'll come, friend." He put his attention back on the game but when he dealt the cards his fingers trembled slightly.

Staffen said, "You ready to go, Jim?"

"Been ready," Cardigan said and turned with him to the door. There he stopped and looked back, saying, "You'll let me know, won't you, Manning? I'll be at the store and if I ain't, just wait around; I'm never gone long."

CHAPTER 12

Smoke Purcell came to town but did not come to the store. Jim Cardigan was a little relieved because he didn't have anything to say to Purcell, and he figured no particular good could come of the meeting.

Purcell's purpose in coming in became obvious by nightfall; he went to the freight agent and tied up the stock cars for another thirty days, and ordered eight more, enough to clog the siding. Then he took five rooms at the hotel, paid them up two weeks in advance, and rode out of town.

None of this made any sense at all to Jim Cardigan; he and Bert Staffen talked about it that evening over supper, and it still didn't make any sense.

When Staffen went home, Cardigan went over to the saloon, had a glass of beer, then walked into the back to Helen Jensen's quarters. He knocked and heard her step as she came to open the door.

Taking off his hat, he said, "Hate to intrude, but it has been some days since I even said hello and . . ."

"Don't stand out there in the hall," she said and stood aside, closing the door after him. She wore a long robe, her hair was long and loose around her shoulders, and he could see that she had been reading. "Want some coffee? Or something stronger?"

"The coffee's fine," Cardigan said and smiled. "I haven't had an urge to—well, I mean that a beer at the end of the day does me just fine." He took off his coat and hat and laid them aside and sat down while she brought him the coffee, and a cup for herself. "Smoke was in town today," he said.

"So I heard."

"He didn't come around?"

"Why should he?" She leaned back in her chair and put her feet on an ottoman and wrapped the robe tightly about her. "Did you come here to talk about him? If you did, you're . . ."

Cardigan shook his head. "No, I didn't come to do that." The whistle of the Cheyenne train came faintly through the walls and he turned his head and looked at the clock on her bureau. "Nearly an hour late," he said.

"Jim, why did you come here?" she asked.

He shrugged and drank some of his coffee, then said, "Maybe I was gettin' so lonesome I couldn't stand it."

"What makes you think I'm good company?"

"Because we both feel a little out of step," Cardigan said. "There ain't much to our lives except a lot of loose ends, and if we was gonna

127

die tomorrow we'd wonder what we'd done with all our chances."

She looked at him a moment, then got up to shake down the fire and remained with her back to him. "You've come close to the truth, Jim. Close enough to hurt. I hate this place. Hate it because it's all I have and twenty years from now I can see myself here, fat, with turkey wattles under my chin, a saloon madam no one wants and everyone tolerates." She turned and looked steadily at him. "And behind me a succession of lovers, none of them good, none of them what I wanted."

"Sell it out," he said. "Take the money and go someplace else and get a new start."

"Don't you think I've thought of that?" She shook her head. "But it's too late for that. A few years too late. I'm past the point where I can start again, alone."

The front door to her place opened and the rush of voices and laughter picked up, making her frown slightly. "Excuse me," she said and stepped out. A moment later, having had her look, she was back. "A bunch came in. Probably off the train."

The laughter of the men came through the walls, a strong, demanding sound, and Jim Cardigan said, "I want a look." He stepped into the short hall and opened the door leading to the bar. They stood in a row, ten strong, all cattlemen in heavy coats and high-crowned hats. The town customers had been pushed back, which was usually the way things

128

went when men like this came to town. Cardigan's first glance was casual, then he recognized the men and said, "Hey, Muley!" and joined them, and they surrounded him and pounded him on the back and fired questions at him so fast he couldn't begin to answer.

With them all talking at once and crowding around him, he put it together piece by piece; Smoke Purcell had hired them, forty a month and found and they'd just arrived on the Cheyenne train and had a big thirst to kill before doing anything.

He had a drink with them to satisfy them, then he took Muley to a table and left the bottle between them. Cardigan laughed and said, "I never thought you'd be interested in sheep, Muley."

"I ain't," he said and grinned. He was a young man, square faced, with a bland, untrimmed mustache. "You and Smoke's got a good thing goin' here, Jim. I like it."

There was the urge in Cardigan to set this man straight, to tell him that he was no longer Smoke Purcell's partner, but an inner caution took hold of him and he decided to let Muley Bates go on thinking what he wanted to think. It was a natural thing for him to do since he had known they were partners, and had worked the same outfit off and on for six years.

"Smoke's pretty sharp," Cardigan admitted. "How does it sound to you?"

"Perfect," Muley said. "I never had any use for sheepmen anyway, and with Smoke holdin' grazin' rights on that high country, we can run cattle in there, push the sheepmen off and never fire a shot." He poured a drink, downed it, and laughed some more. "I got to hand it to Smoke. You know, there was times when I had him down for just a smart kid with sneaky ways, but I've changed my mind. He has got the siding blocked with stock cars to keep the sheepmen from selling off or shippin', and with the law on his side, he can move 'em off that grazin' land." He reached out and slapped Cardigan playfully on the cheek. "Damn it, it's good, you know. We've got four hundred head of maverick stock ready to move on the minute we clear those sheepmen out of there."

"Yeah, we're all gonna be rich," Cardigan said dryly. "You fellas ready for a little shootin', just in case things work out that way?"

Muley Bates patted a bulge under his coat. "We don't figure to have much trouble, Jim. After all, the law's on Smoke's side, ain't it?"

"Smoke thinks of everythin'," Cardigan said. He looked around the saloon and tried to figure out some way to get out without making Muley Bates suspicious. Then he leaned forward and said, "I was just about to get friendly with a certain lady when you fellas came in. Now if I expect to get anywhere . . ."

"Sure," Muley said. "We'll see you out to the place, huh?"

"Yeah," Cardigan said and went into the back.

Helen Jensen was waiting and said, "When I saw that they knew you I stayed out of it. Smoke's friends?"

"Smoke hired 'em," Cardigan said. "I've got to see Bert Staffen. If I come back, can I use the back door?"

She nodded. "Better use it now."

He got his coat and hat and went out and threaded his way through the dark alley and turned onto a side street. Staffen was a widower who lived alone in a small frame house and it was dark when Cardigan went to the door. He knocked for a few moments, then a lamp came on and Staffen called, "Who is it?"

"Jim. I've got to talk to you."

Staffen opened the door and he stepped inside. "Come into the living room; there's some fire left in the stove." He went on ahead and poked the coals and added wood. "You want the lamp on?"

"This is fine," Cardigan said, and told him what Smoke Purcell's plans were as Staffen listened, his expression dark.

When Cardigan was through, Bert Staffen said, "I'm going to get dressed and go out there and try and talk some sense into that fool. He'll have this country in an uproar."

"It'll be after three in the morning time you

131

get there," Cardigan said. "You want to get shot?"

"I'll take Val Sansing along to make this official."

"Then I'd better go too," Cardigan said. "Leastways he knows my voice so there's less chance of someone gettin' hurt."

"All right," Staffen said. "Get three horses and I'll get dressed and wake Val Sansing. Meet us in front of the store in an hour."

Cardigan nodded and left the house and as he walked back toward the stable, he made up his mind. He kept his horse in one of the rear stalls and lit a lantern so he could see to saddle up; in doing so, he burned his hand on the glass for someone had just blown it out. A few minutes later he led his horse to the door and swung up, then rode out of town, taking the road to the Ramey place.

He knew that Staffen would be sore because he'd gone on alone, but he felt strongly about this; he had to give Smoke Purcell one chance no one else would give him. Cardigan figured he owed him that much and, once he paid it, he wouldn't owe him any more. Inside him there was a smoldering anger, a deep resentment because Smoke had used him in the same way he was going to use Harms and Denny and Muley Bates and the others. Cardigan thought of his work building the hoghouses Smoke Purcell never intended to use, and he felt like some child who

132

had been given a useless chore just to keep him out of mischief.

There was no light showing at the Ramey place when Cardigan rode in and dismounted by the porch, but he saw the barn door open and two men standing there and knew that Muley and the others were bedding down there.

Cardigan stepped onto the porch and knocked on the door and in a moment a light came on, then Lila opened the door, her eyes widening in surprise when she saw him.

"I want to talk to Smoke," Cardigan said.

"He's—not here," she said. She wore a long nightgown of thin flannel and he stepped inside and closed the door. "You'd better not come in here," she said. "I'm not dressed."

"I can see that," Cardigan said. "Lila, I've got to see Smoke tonight."

She opened her mouth to tell him again, then Cardigan heard a noise, a bare foot whispering on the floor and he looked past her to the bedroom door to see Smoke Purcell standing there, wearing only the bottom part of his long underwear.

"Well, what do you know," he said and smiled.

Cardigan's glance whipped to Lila Ramey, and she turned her back to him and stayed that way.

"Get back in bed, Lila," Purcell said. "You know how cold your feet get." He stepped aside so she could go past and she closed the door. Purcell then walked over to the stove and rolled a cigarette, taking a match off the top of the shelf for his light.

"So you moved in," Cardigan said. "Did you have to do that?"

"Is that what you want to talk about?" He looked at Cardigan; the marks on his face were still there, faint now, but there to remind Cardigan of how good it had felt to hit him. "Get to the point and get out."

"Smoke, I saw Muley in town."

"So he said."

"I know what you're doin' now."

Purcell shrugged. "What of it?"

"Don't do it," Cardigan said. "As a favor."

"I don't owe you any," Purcell said evenly. "Jim, understand something right now. I'm a big man. You know what I mean? I've got land and a great big grip on this whole thing. And I'm goin' to squeeze it and see what kind of juice comes out."

"What about Lila? She go along with this?"

"Lila's had the little end of the stick too. Time that it's changed." He drew on his cigarette, then his attention sharpened as horsemen rode into the yard.

Cardigan said, "That's Staffen and the sheriff, Smoke. They want to talk too."

"And I don't," Purcell said. "Get 'em out of here."

Cardigan shook his head. "How can I do that, if I wanted to?"

Quickly Purcell went to the bedroom door and opened it. "Come here, Lila. Hurry up." When she came to the door, he took her arm and pulled her to one side so that they couldn't be seen through the window. "Jim, you tell 'em I'm not here."

"I ain't gonna lie for you," Cardigan said.

"You'll do it for her," Purcell said. "When they step inside they're gonna think what you thought. You don't want 'em to think that about her, do you, Jim?" He stepped to the bedroom door and spoke from just inside it. "I'll be under the bed, Jim. You play it smart and no one's goin' to know anything."

Cardigan's face was dark with anger and his mustache seemed to bristle as he bit his lips. "Smoke, suppose I throw her to the dogs?"

"You won't," Purcell said. Steps came across the porch and there was no more time for talk.

Cardigan went to the door and opened it and Staffen and Sansing came in; Staffen's face mirrored his irritation.

"Couldn't you wait?" he asked.

"I had to try it my way," Cardigan said. "Smoke's not here."

"Sorry to intrude, Miss Ramey," Staffen said, taking off his hat. "Where's Purcell?"

"In the high meadows," she said. "Been there for three days. Since he came back from town." She smiled. "Excuse me while I get my robe. It's chilly in here."

"I know you won't mind if I look in there," Val Sansing said and stepped to the bedroom door. He scratched a match and held it high, then turned

135

back and gave Staffen a glance. "Looks like we took a ride for nothing."

"Forgive the intrusion," Staffen said, turning to the door. "Coming, Jim?"

"I asked him to stay for coffee," Lila said quickly. "Won't you . . ."

"Thanks, no," Staffen said. "See you tomorrow, Jim."

They went out and Cardigan stood there until they rode out, then Smoke Purcell came from the bedroom carrying his pistol. "You did that nicely, Jim. Now we can talk."

"There's nothin' to say now," Cardigan said and swung to the door. He put his hand on the knob, then stopped when he heard Purcell cock the gun. He looked back and said, "Put that thing away."

"I want you to stay awhile," Purcell said. "We're goin' to have a party."

CHAPTER 13

Without getting within jumping distance of Jim Cardigan, Smoke Purcell eased around to the door and called out, "Hey! Muley! Bring Stiles and Eddie in here!" Then he stepped back, the gun still pointed at Cardigan's stomach. "You pounded me around a little, Jim. I don't like that."

Lila said, "Smoke, we don't want trouble now."

He laughed and didn't bother to look at her. "Jim knows me too well to think I'd ever let a pushin' around go by, don't you, Jim?"

Muley Bates came in with two men that Cardigan knew casually. Bates smiled and said, "I made a mistake with you, didn't I? Because I just naturally thought you and Smoke—" He shrugged and closed his mouth and looked at Purcell. "Do you really need that gun?"

"Jim's thinkin' about jumpin' me right now, ain't you?" He let the easiness slide out of his voice and his expression turned hard. "Grab him!"

Cardigan anticipated that command, but he was not quick enough, for the three men jumped him and bore him to the floor under their weight and when they hauled him erect, Muley had an arm around his throat and the other two had his arms confined. Smoke Purcell put the pistol away then and walked up to Cardigan and hit him in the mouth. With Muley holding him, there was no way for Cardigan to move his head and absorb the power of the blow. He felt the blood and the roaring in his head, then Purcell laced a punch into his stomach and breathing became an agony for him.

Purcell hit him again to soften him up, then motioned for Muley and the other two to let go. Cardigan tried to stand, but the strength wasn't in him and he fell to his knees, at which Smoke Purcell laughed and went to work in earnest.

Bert Staffen stopped his horse a mile from the Ramey place and took off his gloves to blow on his hands. He said, "Jim should have caught us by now. I'll wait."

Sansing did not argue; he said, "Cardigan can take care of himself, Bert."

"A man can't always do that," Staffen said. "I'll wait a spell until he catches up with us."

"How long is a spell?"

"Until I decide to ride back to the Ramey place and see what's keeping him."

Sansing blew on his hands to warm them, then rolled a cigarette and smoked it half down before speaking. "Purcell wasn't there, so what could be keeping him? The Ramey woman?"

"Purcell was there," Staffen said softly.

Sansing showed an instantaneous resentment. "Now wait a minute, Bert, that's painting the woman pretty black, ain't it? That little statement says a lot and it could hurt her if it got around."

"It's not getting around," Staffen said mildly, "but Purcell has moved into the cabin."

"That's a guess," Sansing said. "Maybe I thought that too, but in my job I have to be absolutely right before I can come to a conclusion like that."

"We've been here a spell," Bert Staffen said. "I'm goin' back."

"All right," Sansing said. "I'll go with you." He turned to his horse, then stopped all movement and held up his hand, listening. The sound came again, of a man's mumbled voice, urging a horse on; Sansing reached under his coat and withdrew his gun from the many folds of his clothing.

"I see him," Staffen said and before Sansing could do anything about it, he started back down the road, afoot, and caught the reins of Cardigan's horse. "Vai! Come here!"

They started to help Cardigan down, but he groaned so that they just struck matches and had a quick look; it was enough to satisfy both of them that they should leave him in the saddle and get him to town as quickly as they could.

As they mounted up, Bert Staffen said, "Do you still think Purcell wasn't there?" He didn't expect Sansing to say anything. "He didn't do this alone either."

"We're wastin' time," the sheriff said and they rode on, keeping Jim Cardigan between them.

They took him to Bert Staffen's house and put

him in the back bedroom and Val Sansing went for the doctor while Staffen got a fire going and washed Cardigan's face the best he could.

The doctor came and Sansing and Bert Staffen went to the parlor for a drink, Staffen walking up and down the room until he began to make the sheriff nervous.

"Can't you sit down?" Val Sansing asked.

"What's taking so long?"

"Sit down and have another drink, Bert." He took out his tobacco and made a smoke, but he took only three puffs off it and shied it into the fire. "I suppose Purcell had a reason for this but I'll be damned if I can see it." He turned his head as the doctor came into the parlor, fingers working on his vest buttons.

"Ah, that's whiskey, isn't it?" He poured some and drank it. "Your friend's in pretty poor shape. Ribs especially. I've got him bound like a barrel. Keep him in bed for two weeks and I'll drop in from time to time to check the cuts on his face." He reached for the bottle again. "It's a wonder he hasn't got a punctured lung." He tossed off his drink and put the glass aside. "Who do I send the bill to?"

"I'll take care of it," Staffen said, and walked the doctor to the door. "Is he awake?"

"Under sedation, but awake," the doctor said. "Goodnight, Bert."

He went out and Staffen walked back down the

hall. As he passed the parlor he nodded and Val Sansing joined him at the bedroom door. They stepped inside and Jim Cardigan moved his head, then raised a hand weakly and waved.

"You look like hell," Staffen said. "Purcell have a little help?"

"Three," Cardigan said, taking care not to move his swollen lips more than necessary. "I made a mistake out there, Bert. Next time I'll be wearin' my gun."

"I looked in the other room," Val Sansing said. "Where was he hiding?"

"Under the bed," Cardigan said.

Staffen laughed softly. "Somehow that fits him." He reached out and patted Jim Cardigan lightly on the shoulder. "I'll send you a nurse."

They went out and Sansing closed the door. He looked at his watch, then blew out a long breath. "This night's about shot. Didn't accomplish much, did we?"

"I see it different," Staffen said softly. "We know just how dangerous a man we're tangling with."

"Mmm," Sansing said, nodding. "Well, good-night."

Helen Jensen came each morning and fixed breakfast for Staffen and Jim Cardigan, and after Staffen left for the store, she stayed on for an hour or so, cleaning up, and talking to Jim Cardigan. She was his contact with everything outside the house, for the saloon was the center of gossip, the focal point of news.

Smoke Purcell wasted no time at all. He served notice on his neighbors to clear out and get their flocks off his grazing land. He didn't need the sheriff to enforce anything for he had his own crew who didn't like sheepmen anyway. The threat of trouble hung like a cloud over them all.

Hot words passed back and forth, and soon open threats. Purcell controlled the railroad siding because he paid demurrage on the stock cars and there was no way for Kline or Means or any of the others to ship even if they could sell. And Purcell had that figured out too. The banker, realizing a good business deal when he saw one, agreed to loan Purcell the money to buy the sheep. Once they had the bill of sale they'd ship and pocket a fat profit.

This was all the seeds anyone needed to start a war, and Cardigan, slowly getting well in Staffen's bed, saw the seeds growing and knew that Purcell and his hired men were putting on the pressure, pushing sheep out of the high pastures, crowding Means and the others until someone would be forced into making a mistake.

Cardigan was back at the store at the beginning of the third week, doing light work, and when he saw Ray Kline come into town he knew it would be Kline who took the step, for Kline was the jumpy one, the one who had shot once before and missed.

Twenty minutes after Kline arrived, a customer dropped into the store and said that Kline was at the saloon and he was calling Purcell out. Someone was already riding to the Ramey place to carry the message and the odds were that by early evening this would be settled, one way or another.

Cardigan and Staffen took their lunch in the saloon and Kline sat at a table alone, a glass of beer in front of him and his shotgun by his right elbow. As soon as they had made sandwiches and ordered beer, they walked over to the table and Staffen said, "Care if we sit down, Ray?"

"Wish you wouldn't," Kline said. "You know I'm expectin' someone, Bert."

"Yes, we know that," Staffen said. "You know Jim Cardigan, don't you?"

Kline nodded and said, "All along I thought you two were some different." He studied Cardigan for a moment. "It was a feelin' I've had, like you could be hurt by seein' another man hurt, troubled when he was troubled. Purcell never cared one way or another. He's hard."

"Too hard for you, Ray," Staffen said gently. "You could never kill a man without hesitating. Purcell won't do that."

"Nothin' holds me back when I'm mad," Kline said. "And I'm mad now."

"Your aim's poor when you're mad," Cardigan said. "Didn't you learn that?" He leaned back in his chair. "Kline, do you think the sheriff's going to allow this?"

"How can he stop it? I do it today, or tomorrow, or next month. Is he goin' to follow me around?" He shook his head. "I've talked to Sansing. He knows he can't stop me." He picked up his beer and took a sip. "I've worked hard all my life for the things I have, and they ain't much. But I'm goin' to lose all that, Bert. Every last bit of it I'm goin' to lose because some tough guy comes into my neck of the woods and steps on me. A man's got more rights than that, ain't he? Hell, who's the law for, me or men like Purcell?" He nodded his head. "Sure, I know I should have filed for grazin' rights on that land, and I would have someday when I had the money. We all would have, but who needed to file when we were all neighbors? All friends."

"Ray, think of your wife and kids," Staffen said.

"I am," Kline said. "Alive, shoved off my land, broke with no hope of ever gettin' to my feet again, what good am I to her then? Bert, sometimes in a man's life, the best thing he can do is maybe to die, or kill off what's puttin' him down." He smiled thinly. "Some years ago I bought insurance, fifteen hundred dollars' worth. I've got my policy over in the bank vault. So win or lose, my family gets a start someplace else. If I kill Purcell, none of us need worry. If it's the other way around—well, like I said, they're cared for and get a new start."

144

Jim Cardigan had been listening carefully. "Kline, you know we're goin' to stop this if we can, don't you?"

"Figured that's what you wanted to talk about."

"Suppose," Bert Staffen said, "I just hauled off and hit you a good lick and took that shotgun away from you?"

"I'd come to sooner or later and get another one," Kline said evenly. "Bert, you've got to understand that I can't be stopped. My sheep are in the high pastures. Ain't moved even one. Don't intend to either. Purcell wants me, he's got to come to me and kill me. He's goin' to get the mark put on him, Bert. One way or another."

"Suppose you kill him," Bert said. "Sansing will arrest you and you'll be tried for it."

"That suits me," Kline said. "Who do you figure in this town would hang me for killin' Purcell? We're all little people, Bert. None of us will ever amount to much. We'll get along and make ends meet but we're not big dreamers. Who'd hang me, Bert?"

Staffen sighed and got up. "I wish you luck, Ray."

He and Cardigan went back to the bar to leave their glasses, then they both went outside. The day was warm with a bright sun melting snow along the edge of the street and making wet spots in the boardwalk.

Val Sansing was standing in front of his office down the street. He looked at them and then nodded

145

his head and went inside; they walked the few steps, went in and closed the door.

"You talked to Kline?" They nodded and he sat down. "So did I. The damn man baffles me. What can I do? Lock him up? He wouldn't care. As soon as I turned him loose he'd get a gun and challenge Purcell again."

"We're taking this from the wrong end," Staffen said. "Let's stop Purcell."

"How? What has he done that's illegal?" Val Sansing shook his head. "I went out there by myself and tried to talk to him. He simply said he's protecting property on which he holds a grazing lease. I can't arrest him for tying up the siding. As long as he pays the bill, the cars can stay there. As for the deal he and the banker have cooked up, it's just good, dirty business. Hell, Kline himself bought his place on a sheriff's sale from a man who'd lost his shirt there. And Purcell's life has been threatened. A man can protect himself." He spread his hands. "I've got to sit here and watch this, then move afterward."

"If there's anyplace to move to," Cardigan said. "Smoke's too smart to make a fool play and get himself hung for it. He has got Kline in his pocket and you know it."

"Damn it, yes, I know it," Sansing said.

CHAPTER 14

Jim Cardigan was boxing grocery orders at the counter and he had a clear view of the street when Smoke Purcell rode into town. Purcell went past and rode on a few yards, then swung his horse around and dismounted outside. He came and stepped up to the counter and said, "I'm glad to see you're learnin' a trade, Jim." He dug into his coat pocket and threw down a grocery list. "Have this ready for me in an hour. Two sacks."

"Smoke, don't kill that man," Cardigan said.

"He wants to kill me," Purcell said. "Jim, he took one shot at me. What am I going to do?"

"Pull out. I'll go with you."

Purcell shook his head. "I don't want to go, Jim." Bert Staffen stepped into the doorway from the back room and watched as Purcell said, "I'll be back in an hour. Have the stuff ready."

He went out and walked on down the street and Staffen took off his sleeve protectors and reached for his coat; as he turned to get it, Cardigan saw the pistol in his back pocket.

"Come on," Staffen said and they went out.

Cardigan buttoned his coat and they hurried to the saloon, pushing aside men who blocked the door. The room was quiet and Purcell was at the bar, ordering his beer; a clear avenue had been made between him and Ray Kline, who still sat at the table.

With the beer in hand, Purcell turned and walked over to Kline and stood with his thighs barely touching the edge of the table. The shotgun lay on the table and Kline did not touch it; the muzzle pointed slightly past Purcell.

"Kline, you're makin' trouble for me."

"I hope so," Kline said softly. He watched as Purcell sipped his beer, put the stein down and rested his hands lightly on the back of a wooden chair. "We could have got along," Kline went on, "but you never wanted that."

"Why should I want it?" Purcell asked. "The first time I ever saw you, you was set to steal me blind. Kline, get off my land. I won't tell you that again."

"I'm not goin'," Kline said. "I'm not going to miss this time either."

His hand slapped against the stock of the shotgun and Purcell jumped back, swung the chair and sent it crashing down. He caught at the shotgun as Kline was lifting it and he smashed it down against the table and both barrels went off, the recoil knocking it out of Kline's hand. For a shocked instant, Kline stared, then tried to get up, knocking over his chair as Purcell's hand went beneath the heavy folds of his coat; he drew his gun and fired as it came level and a surprised, pained look came over Kline's face, then he fell heavily and rolled over on his back.

Smoke Purcell walked around the table and looked at Kline, then he put the gun away and stood there. "Well, where's the marshal?" he asked. "Let's get this over with so I can go home." He looked around, then turned and walked out, but stopped when he got to the porch because Val Sansing was there.

"I'll take your gun," Val Sansing said evenly.

"Why, sure," Purcell said, handing it over.

"Let's go to my office," Sansing said and walked slightly behind Purcell all the way down the street. Cardigan and Staffen came out, paused a moment, then went on to the store.

When they were hanging up their coats, Staffen said, "Val can't hold him and he knows it. Kline had a shotgun and made his intentions plain. He fired twice before Purcell did." He slapped his hands together. "But there was nothing fair about it. We all know it."

"The others will move now," Cardigan said. "He'll have his way." He picked up Purcell's grocery list and started to stack goods on the counter. "We didn't do anything to stop him, Bert, and we both had guns." He looked at Staffen. "I haven't been drunk for some months, but I feel like it now."

The doorbell jangled and Pete Manning came in, followed by Rand, who went over to the stove to stand and warm his hands. Manning bought some cigars and lit one, then said, "The sheepherder

149

was a fool." He shrugged. "But then, most dead men are, wouldn't you say?" He smiled and looked at Jim Cardigan. "I was crossing over from the hotel when I saw your partner ride into town and stop here. I thought that since his horse is tied out front, he would likely stop here before going back."

"So?" Cardigan asked.

"So I want to talk to him," Manning said pleasantly. "I feel that Purcell has been neglecting me. That makes me sad."

Cardigan looked at Rand's expressionless face. "Does it make you sad too?" He knew the man wouldn't answer, yet he didn't care.

Taking the cigar from his mouth, Manning said, "Cardigan, I'm afraid that you've forced Rand into an active dislike of you. Why do you want to make enemies?"

"Because I don't need any more friends," Cardigan said. He looked at Rand again. "Did you get your hands warm yet? Got them all limbered up for a real fast shoot after you chivvy Purcell into goin' for his gun?" He saw a flicker of interest in the man's eyes and came around the counter and faced Rand. "Out of the store. The heat's for the customers to soak up."

He looked at Rand's eyes and saw the muddy depths of them and knew that he was pushing dangerously hard, yet he felt a surge of excitement in him, a breathlessness, as though he had just broken a particularly fine horse.

150

Suddenly he raised his arm and jammed it against Rand's throat, shoving the man back, forcing his buttocks and back thighs against the hot stove. Rand's hand darted to his gun and he actually drew it before the pain hit him and he screamed and dropped the gun and his body went into a tight bow, away from the searing heat.

The gun went off when it hit the floor and there was a crash of glass from somewhere behind Cardigan but he did not look around. He jammed up with his knee, caught Rand in the crotch and pushed harder, forcing him against the stove again. Rand's eyes were wide, distended eggs and his mouth was opening and he gurgled deep in his throat, trying to strain away from Cardigan.

Then he caught Rand by the scruff of the neck, spun him away from the stove, and hit him flush in the mouth, knocking him down. Rand rolled and started to get up, but Cardigan swung his foot, catching the man alongside the head, driving him down again. Then before Rand could roll or get up, Cardigan stepped on his gunhand and put his weight on the boot heel. Rand screamed when the bones broke, and rolled on the floor, clutching his hand to his stomach, all bent over as though he were trying to hide it.

Only then did Cardigan turn to pick up Rand's gun and look at Bert Staffen; the storekeeper stood on the near side of the counter, one of Pete Manning's arms in his twisting grip.

There was a smear of blood on Manning's head and scattered glass on the floor and Cardigan knew that Manning had been hit with a bottle.

"You damned near got jumped from behind," Bert Staffen said. He freed Manning and gave him a shove. "Take your boy and get out of my store. You want to gun somebody, then figure on doing it somewhere else."

Manning straightened his arm and rubbed the muscle; he looked at Rand, still moaning on the floor, then at Jim Cardigan. "Did you have to cripple him?"

"Ain't it better than killin' him?" Cardigan walked over and opened the door. "You've been invited. Do I have to throw you out on your ass?"

A firm step outside caused Manning to hesitate. It was Val Sansing, who stepped in, looked once at Rand, then at Manning and sized the whole thing up in an instant. "Manning, you damned fool!" he said.

Rand groaned when Manning lifted him and helped him out, headed for the doctor's office. Sansing closed the door, his glance going to Jim Cardigan. "He beats the hell out of you and you stick up for him. Why?"

"He wouldn't have had a chance with Rand."

"That didn't hold you back," Sansing said.

"I didn't use a gun."

"You don't make sense. Why didn't you stick up for Kline?" He waved his hand, indicating he didn't want an answer, then took off his hat and scratched his head. "Why in hell didn't I go into the meat-packin' business like my father wanted me to?"

Smoke Purcell came down the street and got his horse. He saw them standing inside the store but did not come in; he just mounted up and rode out of town.

"Now there's gratitude," Bert Staffen said.

"He don't know what it means," Val Sansing said. "I told him to watch himself, but he won't. His kind never does." He put his hat back on his head and buttoned his coat. "They always leave the body for me to take home, and there's always a wife to tell that there's not a damned thing that can be done about it." He looked at them and walked out. Cardigan got a broom and swept up the glass and picked up Rand's gun.

It was a beautiful weapon, a nickel-plated .45 and he unloaded it and tried the action a few times and found it velvet smooth, the trigger pull light and delicate. He put the gun on the counter and said, "There wasn't much more to him than that, was there?"

"He misjudged you," Staffen said. "You know, Jim, I have a theory about that. I don't think it's the man with the badge and the gun who's going to bring peace. Oh, I grant you it's the man with the badge and the gun who'll keep the peace, but it's the man without either who'll get there in the first place. You take Rand, for example. He didn't know exactly what to do with you, and while he was making up his mind, he got lumped out of shape. You see the gist of my theory? How do you fight a determined, unarmed man? You beat him up and he gets over it and comes at you again. If you kill him it's murder and you get a rope around the neck." Bert Staffen shook his head. "My father had a store in Kansas during the cattle-drive days and he never carried a gun in his life, yet he could handle anything that could walk through his door."

Cardigan went behind the counter and started taking groceries out of the sacks and putting things back on the shelves. He said, "I didn't think Smoke really wanted to order anything."

"Well," Staffen said wryly, "I see that he can't lie to you and get away with it any more."

Kline's family came to town three days later, settled a bill at the store, then bought a railroad ticket and went to the depot to wait. Joe Harms and Mort Denny came in later, went to the saloon for their drink, then walked to the depot at train time to see the Kline family off, as though they had to see how sad a thing this was, a kind of rehearsal for the time when they'd be doing the same thing.

Harms came into the store just before closing with his grocery list and sad face. "A terrible thing," he told Staffen. "Undermines a man's respect for the law." He saw Cardigan in the back room and shot him a dark glance. "Funny you'd keep him around here, Bert."

"He's the best man I ever had," Staffen said. "You want anything else, Joe?"

He didn't and went out, heading up the street to the saloon.

Cardigan went and had his supper and came back so that Staffen could eat. While Staffen was out, Muley Bates and three of his friends rode into town, a little pay in their pocket and a thirst for whiskey. Cardigan was outside, moving some display barrels in when they rode by and Muley wheeled his horse, circled back and came right up on the walk, meaning to crowd Cardigan, who lifted a broom and shoved the straw against the horse's muzzle. The animal shied away and got off the walk. Muley checked the animal's alarm, laughed and said, "You never did scare worth a damn," and rode on to the saloon.

Cardigan finished his work and waited on a few late customers, by which time Staffen was back. They counted the money and were getting ready to close the store when down the street there was a sudden whooping and feet pounded out a dead run along the boardwalk.

"You get cattlemen in a town and you've got noise," Staffen said, looking up as his door burst open and Harms and Denny poured into the room.

"They're after us!" Denny yelled and jumped over the counter.

There wasn't time to think or to ask questions; both Staffen and Cardigan ran toward the door, Cardigan swooping up a pickax handle from a handy barrel of them. One of the men chasing Harms and Denny boldly rode his horse right through the door and Cardigan swung the ax handle, cracking the horse a glancing blow on the muzzle.

The animal screamed in pain and reared and the rider was caught brutally between the horse's neck and the low doorjamb. Cardigan heard bone break, then the horse backed out, but the rider sagged off, falling so that he lay half inside and half outside the store.

Muley Bates and the others had been crowding in, and they swung down and ran forward, Muley bending over the fallen man. He started to lift him but the man's head rolled around loosely and Bates slowly lowered him.

He looked at Jim Cardigan and said, "You broke his neck."

"I hit the horse, and it reared," Cardigan said flatly. "It was an accident."

"You had no call to hit anythin'," Bates said angrily.

A crowd was forming outside and Val Sansing was swearing his way through it; he came up, took a quick look, then saw Harms and Denny peeking from behind the counter. "You two go on home. Go on now." He swung around and faced

Muley Bates. "What the hell did you think you were goin' to do?"

"Aw, nothin', really," Bates said. "There was no call to kill Pokey."

Bert Staffen said, "The damned fool tried to ride his horse into the store. Jim was closest so he hit the horse with an ax handle. The animal reared and the rider got rapped against the top of the door. It was an accident."

Val Sansing nodded. "That's good enough for me. All right, everyone clear out!"

Muley Bates's face was dark with anger. "That's all? What kind of law is there around here anyway?" He pointed to Jim Cardigan. "He may think that's all, but I don't."

"I said it was over," Sansing repeated softly. "Now if you've got a brain in your head you'll take your friend and get out of town." He stood there, staring at Muley Bates, and finally the man made a cutting motion with his hand and turned away.

They took the dead man and put him across his horse, then Muley came back. He looked at Sansing and Cardigan, and at Bert Staffen. "We was just havin' some fun. We'll go now, but we'll come back, and when we do, we'll have some fun with you."

He wheeled and jumped on his horse and they rode out of town, making no noise at all.

CHAPTER 15

Each day the snow receded under the warming spring sun and water ran in the gutters along the main street, which was a bed of mud, and on the back-street lawns, grass pushed up in thick green tufts. The winter was dying and the birds came back and once in awhile something happened that got everyone to talking; like the day Smoke Purcell went to the bank and met Harms and Means there, and the others, and when it was over, Purcell and the banker had bought the sheep and shipped them and his crew stayed in town to celebrate. Harms and his friends went on home, but it was only a gesture and everyone knew it for they had been cleaned out; what small flocks they could graze on their own property wouldn't support them and it would just be a matter of time before they were forced to sell everything.

Cardigan expected Purcell to come to the store, but he didn't; he sent Muley Bates in to do the ordering. Bates's eyes were cold and remote because he still hadn't figured out who was really to blame for Pokey's death. Cardigan expected Bates to start something, but he didn't; he loaded the order onto a wagon and drove out.

Val Sansing was especially watchful during those times when Purcell and his crew were in town, but he couldn't do a thing about the kind of trouble Purcell was making, because Purcell never made a move unless he had the law on his side. He didn't bother the sheep ranchers or put a foot on their property or allow any of his hired men to do so, and he didn't seem to care what the town thought of him.

He went where he pleased and did what he pleased and when Helen Jensen ordered him out of her place, he just laughed, finished his drink and left.

Rand took to carrying a sawed-off shotgun when his hand healed stiff and he still stood behind Pete Manning while the game was going on. At other times he would stand outside the saloon, looking up and down the street and when he saw Cardigan, his eyes would follow him until he passed out of sight, as though he were waiting for the exact time to make his move.

Most of the people in town went to the stock-yard siding to see Purcell's shorthorns the day they arrived. Bates and his crew tallied the shipment, then drove them on to the Ramey place. Only people didn't call it that any more, it was the Purcell place now. People seemed eager to forget about Lila Ramey, who hadn't come to town since the fire; most everyone knew that she shared the house with Smoke Purcell.

Cardigan and Bert Staffen were still eating lunch together in Helen Jensen's place, and finally Val

Sansing got into the habit of making it four around the table, and they were all four there, finishing one of Helen's pies, when a man came in, walked over to the table and said to no one in particular, "Guess who just came to town."

"You tell me," Sansing said.

"The Ramey woman," the man said and went to the bar to kill his thirst.

Sansing got up from the table and walked to the front door, looked out for a moment, then came back and sat down. "She just went up the stairs to Doc Cavanaugh's office," he said and sat down, a frown wrinkling his forehead.

Helen Jensen said, "You'd never think it, but I've developed a severe pain in the side."

"Maybe it was the pie," Cardigan said.

Staffen glanced at him, then laughed. "You're not going to get anywhere with that kind of talk." His glance touched Helen Jensen. "A woman's curiosity?"

"A girl like Lila Ramey doesn't live with a man without it tearing her apart. I'll see you later. Stop in for a beer around suppertime." She left them and crossed the street, using the planks at each corner but still muddying her button shoes. At the top of the stairs she wiped her feet on a mat and went into Cavanaugh's waiting room, showing no surprise at finding Lila Ramey waiting there.

"The street is certainly a mess, isn't it?" Helen said.

Lila Ramey turned her head, then nodded and looked away.

"I like the spring though," Helen said. "The mud washes off and pretty soon it dries up and the flowers bloom. You look a little pale. I always need a purge in the spring. You get kind of closed in during the winter and need an airing out. You know?"

Cavanaugh came up the stairs and opened the door. "Sorry I wasn't in," he said. "Who's first?"

Lila Ramey got up and Cavanaugh opened the door to his examination room and she went in. Helen Jensen sat there for ten minutes. Now and then she could hear the soft run of Cavanaugh's voice, then she heard Lila Ramey crying.

She got up and quietly went down the stairs, crossed the street and entered Staffen's store. Cardigan was waiting on a customer and Bert was in the back room. Helen went straight there and as soon as Cardigan was finished he joined them.

"Well?" Staffen said.

"Why would a woman cry in a doctor's office?" Helen asked.

"You tell me," Staffen said. "You're a woman."

"Because she's pregnant," Helen Jensen said, as both men looked at each other with their mouths open. "Do you know of a better reason?"

"I don't know any reasons," Cardigan said softly. "But you're not sure."

"I'm sure enough to bet my place, lock, stock, and barrel, against your pay this week," Helen

Jensen said. "Somebody ought to shoot Smoke Purcell. She can't handle a thing like this. Few women can." She turned to the door, stopping when Cardigan spoke.

"What are you goin' to do now?"

"Help her, if she'll let me," Helen said and went out.

She recrossed the street and waited at the foot of the stairs. Finally Lila Ramey came out and was halfway down before she saw Helen Jensen standing there. She stopped and made a slight turn as though to retreat upstairs again.

"Why don't you come over to my rooms and have some coffee?" Helen suggested.

"I—no thank you."

Helen looked at her, then said, "Lila, the walls in Cavanaugh's office aren't very thick." She hated to do this, to hit her so hard, but there didn't seem to be any other way. She watched Lila turn pale and put her hand to her mouth.

"Oh, dear God," she said.

Helen went up the steps and took her arm. "Come on and have the coffee. This is a woman's business anyway."

They went across the street and through the saloon and Helen Jensen closed the door and put on the coffeepot. She took Lila's coat and hung it up, then sat down.

"What do I do?" Lila Ramey asked in a small voice.

"You don't waste any time," Helen said. "People like to count and even though they come up with some months shy, you'll be married and that takes the sting out of it."

Lila Ramey looked up. "He has what he wants. Why should he marry me?"

"Oh, now, Smoke's a dog, but he wouldn't do that," Helen said. Then her manner sobered quickly. "Have you told him, Lila?"

She nodded and looked at her folded hands. Helen waited a moment, then got up and walked around the room. "There's no need to tell me what he said. I can guess."

"He didn't say anything," Lila said. "He just laughed."

Helen turned to see Lila's eyes brim with tears. Yet she had herself under control. "I thought he loved me. He said that he loved me. What did he mean when he said that, Helen?"

"Who knows what he meant?" She went to the stove and got the coffee and poured two cups. "Are you going back to him?"

There was a long silence. Then Lila said, "I still love him. And I don't have any other place to go."

"Then stay here," Helen said. "Please."

"Why would you want me to do that?" Lila asked.

For a moment Helen hesitated, then she said, "Because I could have saved you all of this, Lila. I could have come to you and told you the truth.

163

But you probably wouldn't have believed me. Anyway, I should have tried, and I didn't."

"What could you have said?"

"That Smoke once spent the night here."

Helen watched the break in Lila Ramey's expression and smiled, "See, even now you don't want to believe it." She sighed and sat down and lifted her coffee cup. "Even now you can't bring yourself to hate him because you can't believe that any man you loved could be all bad. That's a common mistake women make, Lila. And how they pay for it!"

"I don't know," Lila said. It was as though she hadn't heard the other woman and was talking to herself. "I just don't know what I should do."

Helen said quickly, "Why don't you go in the bedroom and stretch out for a spell. I'll be back."

She left and went back to Staffen's store and found Cardigan and Staffen taking inventory; they stopped work and sat on some crates. "I can see that you were right," Staffen said. "When's the wedding?"

"There ain't goin' to be any weddin'," Cardigan said. "Can't you tell?"

"He laughed at her," Helen said. "Jim . . ."

"I know. I've got to do somethin'." He spread his big hands. "What? Give me a hint."

"Talk to him, if you can."

"Now, Helen, you just damn well know talking

isn't going to shift Purcell one way or the other. Can't she go back to him? Did he throw her out?"

"That's a helluvan attitude," Helen said, with some heat. "That woman's going to have a baby!"

"Women do," he said tartly.

She flounced out, for once at a loss to cope.

Cardigan made a cigarette and lit it. "For God's sake, what does she want me to do? What would I say to Smoke? This isn't my business and I've got no right to make it my business."

"You're right, of course," Staffen soothed him. "But women don't see things that way. Not when it comes to having kids." He ruminated a while, then offered, "Maybe we should talk to Lila? Maybe it wouldn't do any good, but on the other hand, we don't really know how she feels."

Jim nodded a gloomy assent.

The two men slowly made their way over to the saloon. There, both downed a quick shot before making their way to the back room. Staffen knocked and they stood, uneasily waiting. When Helen came to the door, she regarded them sourly.

"Well?"

Bert cleared his throat. Jim said carefully, "Like to talk with Lila, Helen. There may be something I can do."

From inside the room there was the sound of quiet crying. Jim gently pushed past Helen and went to the girl.

"Lila? Now come on, girl. Quit that. You're acting

as though you hadn't any friends. Lila, we got on pretty good together when I was out to your place. I reckon we were straight with each other and you know I'd have admired to do anything for you I could. Now that hasn't changed any. You want to have me talk to Smoke, why, I'll just do my best to get him to marry you . . ."

Behind him he heard Helen's indignant snort and wished fervently he'd kept his mouth shut. But Lila had raised a wet, swollen face. "It's not the marrying I care about so much," she said. "It's being with Smoke!"

"You mean he doesn't want you back?"

She shook her head. "He wants me, all right," she said. "But I'm afraid . . ." She stopped.

"Afraid of what, Lila?" His voice was very gentle.

"That he'll be killed," she said flatly. "I can't help it. I've got to tell you. Oh, Jim, he's riding on the sheepmen. He says they're not moving out fast enough and he wants the bottomland. He wants everything. Jim, can you stop him?"

"I guess I'm going to have to try," Cardigan said and turned to the door. "She'll stay here?" He asked this of Helen Jensen.

"She's not going anyplace," Helen said. "Take Val Sansing with you."

"I was going to do that," Cardigan said and went out.

He went to the store first and found Staffen had retreated there. He was finishing with a customer.

Cardigan went behind the counter and got out his cartridge belt and pistol and buckled it on.

"What's going on, Jim?" Staffen asked.

He told the man and Staffen's face turned grave.

"You're going to have company," he said and went to the rifle rack and took down a new Winchester and then got two boxes of shells down from the ammunition shelves.

Armed, they went down the street to Val Sansing's office and found him asleep. He woke when Staffen closed the door, and straightened when he saw they were armed.

"Smoke and his bunch are going to raid Means and the others," Cardigan said. "I don't think there's time to get up a posse."

"Where's he going first?" Sansing said, taking down a rifle.

"I don't know. He's counting on having a clean run at it."

Sansing smiled thinly. "We can't let him get away with that."

They went together to the stable and got horses and mounted up and rode out of town. Sansing took the lead, and set the pace, trying to cover ground as fast as possible without killing the horses.

Cardigan wondered if either Sansing or Bert Staffen really understood what they were facing. Purcell and his bunch were cattlemen and their thinking was as narrow and stubborn as a cattleman can get, feeling that they were the strong ones, the right ones, and devil take the man who got in their way.

Sansing left the road and they cut across the valley. It was a guess on Sansing's part, but he headed for the Harms place. Even before they reached it they could see the pall of smoke rising, being bent by the wind.

When they reached the yard they found the barn fired and already to the ground. Two small outbuildings were burning fiercely but the cabin was intact.

Harms's older boy was in the yard, dead, and they flung off and approached the cabin, guns drawn. Sansing went in first because he was the law. They found Joe Harms in the kitchen, wounded, bleeding badly, but alive.

His rifle was nearby, and it had been fired; Cardigan checked it and found two cartridges in the chamber. Staffen and the sheriff were lifting Harms, getting him onto the bed.

"Where's the rest of your family?" Staffen asked. "Harms, where's your wife?"

The man waved his hand feebly and Cardigan stepped outside. He had a look in all directions, then he saw them, some distance away, a woman and a small boy, running toward the cabin. When they got there, the woman pushed past him and went into the cabin, her crying a strong, tearing sound in the stillness.

Cardigan kept the boy outside; he was six or so

and gangly. "How come you and your ma were away from the house?" he asked.

"They sent us away," the boy said. He kept trying to look past Cardigan, to see into the cabin, but Cardigan held him by the shoulders. "You know these men?"

"They had horses and burned the barn," the boy said.

Sansing came out and blew out a long breath. "He may live." Then he looked at the boy. "Go in and help your ma. Do as she says." And he looked at the other boy, dead in the yard. "We can't even spare the time to bury him."

They turned when Bert Staffen came out. "I'm ready. Are you?"

"We were waiting for you," Cardigan said and mounted his horse.

CHAPTER 16

Clyde Means's place lay a few miles to the west and they cut across the valley toward it, riding three abreast, keeping their horses at a trot and not slacking off until they saw the buildings. The only sign of smoke was what came from the chimney and when they rode into the yard, Means came out, a long-barreled repeating rifle in his hands. When he saw who they were he placed the gun against the side of the house and walked to the well where they were dismounting.

"I wasn't expectin' you all," Means said dryly. "Come inside. There's eats. We're all inside."

"You're expecting trouble then?" Sansing said.

"Sheriff, I've been suspectin' it since Purcell moved into this valley." He shook his head sadly. "It has been a bad winter."

He turned and walked to the house and Sansing said, "You know about Harms then?"

"Don't know nothin' about anybody but myself," Means said. "I got my notice same as the others, I guess."

"What notice?" Staffen asked.

"You'll see," Means said and stepped inside. His wife was at the stove, making a stew; her face had a drawn, worried cast to it. Means's boys, even the smallest, were posted at the windows and they were all armed. "Put out some extra plates, Ruth," Means said and went to the mantel and brought back a piece of paper; he handed it to Val Sansing and stood there as though waiting for an opinion. Sansing read it and handed it to Cardigan:

Sheepmen—
You get one warning. If your dogs bring down one more calf, we'll ride on you and give you the trouble you've been looking for.

Purcell Ranch

"Did your dogs kill a calf?" Sansing asked.

"Hell, no," Means said. "If there was a calf pulled down, a cat likely done it. Sheep attract cats. I got three dogs and they've been around the place." He wiped a hand across his mouth and showed his worry. "That ain't addressed to me personal so I figured they lost some calves and just sent those around to all of us. You said somethin' about Harms?"

"When did you get this note?" Sansing asked.

"Yesterday. You fellas ain't said about Harms," Means reminded them.

Sansing blew out a long breath. "Harms is wounded. His older boy is dead. Purcell and his bunch hit the place. The woman and the other kid were away from the house when it happened." He looked at Cardigan, then at Means. "I think we'll ride on right after supper. Call it a hunch, but I think Purcell did what he intended to do."

Means said, "I guess Harms's dogs . . ."

"It wasn't Harms's dogs," Cardigan said. "That's an excuse. Smoke had this all figured out." He looked at Staffen and the sheriff. "You know what I'm talking about."

They nodded and Val Sansing said, "We'll pay Purcell a visit. He's expecting me." Then a sharpness came into his expression. "That's it exactly. He's expecting me, one man, not you two. Can you see why?"

"It went a little fast for me," Staffen admitted. He looked at Jim Cardigan. "Do you know?"

"I know Smoke," Cardigan said, nodding. "Yes, he's going to kill you, Val. And he'll cover it up. How do you suppose it'll go? Harms's dog killed a calf? They trailed the blood and Harms made a fight of it?" He shrugged. "And when you come around, they'll open up on you and claim afterward that they thought you was Means or one of the Dennys trying to pot-shoot 'em. Who'd stand up and call 'em a liar? And who'd be the law, Val?"

"I never knew a man who could do a thing like that," Means said honestly. He looked from one to the other. "You three fellas—" Then he closed his mouth a moment. "I ain't real brave, but I'll go with you."

"No," Sansing said. "I want you to stay out of it. You've got your family, Clyde. Your place is here."

172

Means nodded and looked at Jim Cardigan. "I never thought you was like him. Didn't know what you was, but it wasn't like him. What makes a fella like that, mister?"

Jim Cardigan thought about it, then said, "I guess he just can't stand bein' nothin'."

Means's wife was setting the table and the four men ate while the boys watched at the windows, and there was little talk. Afterward, Sansing got up and went to the stove for a match to light his cigar. He said, "We thank you for the hospitality, Clyde, but we've got to be going. It'll be dark by the time we reach Purcell's place as it is."

"I understand," Means said and went outside with them and watched them mount up.

As they moved away from Means's yard, Val Sansing said, "Purcell expects me to come alone, and that's the way we'll do it." He took his rifle out of the boot and handed it to Cardigan, along with a box of shells. "Let me have your pistol. I'll give you time to circle and cover the yard the best you can. When the fireworks start, I'll try to make it to some cover. You understand?"

"The three of us ought to go in together," Staffen said.

"We'll do it my way," Val Sansing said.

They rode on through the gathering darkness and stopped away from the ranch; lamps made yellow squares of the windows and a man walked from the barn to the house carrying a lantern. Jim

Cardigan said, "Let me go around on the north side and take a place near those trees. That way I can cover the porch and the side windows of the house. If we have to go in, I'll go first because I know it better than you two do."

"I'll cover the barn on the near side," Staffen said. "That'll give me a crossfire with Jim in the yard and porch."

"Let's hope our luck holds," Sansing said and motioned for them to move out.

Jim Cardigan swung wide, found a place to tie his horse and went the rest of the way on foot, circling the house and taking a position in some trees near the edge of the yard. He could see all of the front of the house and the yard from the corner of the barn to the porch and he hunkered down, the rifle across his lap.

He waited a few minutes, then Sansing rode slowly into the yard and stopped some distance from the porch. The front door opened and Smoke Purcell stepped out; he left the door open and a shaft of yellow light struck Sansing's horse on the chest.

"Come on in, Sheriff," Purcell said. "I'm lonesome for company."

There was another man in the house, Jim Cardigan knew; they had seen him cross the yard with the lantern, and he looked at the front windows and detected a shadow standing back out of Val Sansing's view. Cardigan knew what was

174

going to happen and he left his place and trotted around until he came up against the flank of the house by a window. He looked in and saw Muley Bates standing there, a pistol in his hand, and a wide grin on his face.

Cardigan could hear Sansing's voice, smooth and easy and not at all raised. "I've got to talk to your boys, Purcell. You made a bad mess over at Harms's place."

"I guess we did," Purcell said. "Likely we'll make another."

Cardigan watched Muley Bates and when the man dissolved the window with the barrel of his pistol, Cardigan poked the muzzle of the rifle through the glass and shot Muley Bates through the head. The boom of the shot had hardly faded when Bates fell half through the window to dangle there like a coat thrown over the back of a chair; someone opened up from the vicinity of the barn and Purcell started to back into the house but Cardigan shot right through the door, surprising him, driving him back onto the porch.

Val Sansing flung himself off his horse as a bullet caught the animal and it rolled; he was clear and dashing for the stone well curbing. Cardigan had to make up his mind whether he should go after Purcell or break away from the house and support Bert Staffen, who was trying to hold down the rest of the crew in the barn. The decision wasn't hard and Cardigan ran around the building and crouched down by the corner, pumping three fast shots into the barn.

It was a good cross fire, but it left a flank wide open and Purcell took his chance and ran off the porch and made the darkness beyond the house. Bert Staffen had stopped shooting, then he fired again from a new position near the far corner of the barn.

He was trying to slip in close and Cardigan had to support him. He whistled, caught Sansing's attention, and motioned toward the barn, then he boldly sprinted across the front of the yard, drew some wild, rapid fire, and ended panting against the north wall of the barn.

With Sansing behind the curbing and squarely facing the door, and Staffen and Cardigan at each corner, there was just no way out for the men inside, except through the front and with their hands up.

It was Val Sansing's show, and he called out, "You can't fight your way out of this one and see the sun tomorrow! There's one door and it's covered by me in front and two men with rifles at each corner! You can only shoot at one of us at a time, so figure it out for yourself!"

Cardigan heard a horse and for a moment he couldn't figure it, then he realized that Purcell had found where he had tied his animal up and was getting away. He opened his mouth to yell just as the barn door flew open and two pistols and a rifle sailed out.

Sansing said, "Light a lantern and hold it over your heads. If anyone's holding out a gun, he won't live long."

The lantern was lighted and another pistol came arcing out. Then they stepped out, hands over their heads, and Cardigan and Bert Staffen closed in from both sides.

One of the men called Texas Al said, "I might have known you'd be here, Jim. Where's Muley?"

"Dead," Cardigan said. "But he died enjoyin' himself."

Sansing searched them carefully, then Bert Staffen got a rope from the barn and cut it into lengths and tied their hands behind their backs.

The men looked at each other, then Texas Al said, "It do look suspiciously like we're under arrest for somethin'. You mind sayin' what, Sheriff?"

"Tell me you don't know," Sansing said flatly. "Which one of you killed the Harms boy?"

Again they exchanged glances and Texas Al said, "Muley done it."

"That's right," another said. "Muley did all the shootin'."

"And you all stood around and watched?" Staffen said.

They nodded and admitted that this was so, and Val Sansing said, "My horse is dead. Bring me one of theirs, Bert."

"Smoke found where I tied mine," Cardigan said. "So I'll borrow yours, Bert."

"Now wait a minute," Sansing said. "We came together, and we'll leave together."

"Then you'll have to catch me," Cardigan said. "Or fight me, Val, and I don't think you want to do that."

"He can't get so far that you can't wait a few minutes," Staffen said. "Jim, Purcell's like most men who get too hungry; they go too far and then it just isn't one man's job to stop them. Now we're going to mount up the prisoners and go back to town and put 'em in jail. Then we're going to get Smoke Purcell."

"If he has skipped the county . . ."

"If he has, Jim," Sansing said, "then we'll circulate a Wanted poster on him and figure he'll get caught. But I don't think he'll skip the county. I don't believe you think he will either."

"No," Cardigan said, "he'll have to get me. Even as a gangling kid, he always resented owin' me anything. And this is somethin' he'll want to pay off."

He helped Staffen with the horses and then they mounted the prisoners, with two riding double, swung up and started back to town, the prisoners following Sansing, but guarded at the rear by Jim Cardigan and Bert Staffen.

Finally Staffen said, "Jim, did he really think he could get away with it?"

"He might," Cardigan said. "When you think about it, what would have stopped him, Bert?

178

Sansing would have been dead, and if we elected another sheriff the next day, what could be proved? They had their stories all made up. If it came to trial, do you think you could find a jury who'd want to risk . . ."

"I know," Staffen said. He let the silence run awhile. Then he looked at Cardigan. "Jim, you don't want to kill Purcell."

"I don't want to kill anybody," Cardigan said. "He was my partner a long time, Bert. I've taken sass off him and lumps from him and I've covered his little tricks and saved his job a couple of times but it ain't all been one-sided. Some men can just never settle for what they have, or be happy with what they are and Smoke was like that. He liked to stomp his feet when he walked, soundin' big, you know. He's just a kid, sort of."

"If Sansing can take him alive, he'll try to get him hung," Staffen said. "That's the way it has got to be, Jim."

"I know," Cardigan said. "I hope he puts up a fight. Smoke just wouldn't want to die at the end of a rope."

"It's a little late to decide that now," Staffen said dryly. "I've got no sympathy for the man. And you're wastin' yours, Jim."

"Sure, I know that, but I guess it's all I ever had to offer him. Besides, I started out to stop him for Lila's sake, really. Seems I just can't do anything right when it comes to Smoke."

CHAPTER 17

Val Sansing herded his men into the small jail and came out and got back up on his horse. Then he rode slowly to the end of the main street and when he stopped, Jim Cardigan and Bert Staffen came up and sided him. They sat their horses and looked the length of the street. There were a few horses tied farther down, and a wagon in front of Staffen's store, but the only man in sight was Rand, and he stood across the street from the saloon, the sawed-off shotgun in the crook of his arm.

"He's here," Staffen said softly. "Rand wouldn't be standing there if he wasn't."

Sansing said, "Jim, you go through the alley and cover the other end of the street. Bert, I want you to stay here."

"We started together," Jim Cardigan said, "and we'll finish it together." He looked at Sansing and for a moment the sheriff teetered on the verge of argument, then he nodded and they rode on and dismounted in front of Helen Jensen's place and paused on the walk a moment, having a final look at the street.

Then Cardigan crossed the street to where Rand stood and said, "Have you seen him?"

"If I'd seen him," Rand said, "he'd be dead." His

voice was low and soft and he looked at Cardigan with his flat, expressionless eyes.

"Why don't you be smart and stay out of this?" Cardigan asked.

"Because I was paid to do a job," Rand said. "And when I've earned my money, I'll come after you. That I'll do for nothing."

"You want me to tell Sansing you said that?"

"Tell him what you please," Rand said. "The law doesn't scare me." He raised his right hand, showing Cardigan the stiff and crooked fingers. "For ten years now this has been my fear, that I'd somehow hurt my hands. You didn't have to do this to me." He let his hand drop. "It's the same as cuttin' off a man's arm."

"You've got a mixed-up head," Cardigan said and went back to where Staffen and the sheriff waited. They went inside and the bartender was cleaning up; there was no trade at all. Pete Manning sat at one of the tables, idly working at a game of solitaire. Helen Jensen stood at the far end of the bar and Lila Ramey sat at a corner table, a half-eaten ham sandwich in front of her.

For a moment no one said anything, then Bert Staffen walked over to the bar and said, "Draw three beers, Herbie." Then he turned and hooked his elbows on the bar and looked at Pete Manning. "Did you tell Rand to wait across the street?"

"It was his idea," Manning said. "But I didn't argue with him."

"Where's Smoke Purcell?" Val Sansing asked.

"Come and gone," Manning said. He turned his head and looked at the wall clock. "Almost fifteen minutes now. Too bad you missed him."

"He's still in town?" Cardigan asked.

Manning nodded. "He left a message for you. He wants to say goodbye." He looked at Cardigan and smiled. "You know what he means? He wants to dissolve a partnership, for good."

Lila Ramey locked her fingers together and said, "You're hunting him like animals. That killer waiting across the street and the three of you in here. And *you*." She looked at Jim. "You I trusted. You were going to help . . ." She looked as though she was on the verge of tears and stopped talking.

"Purcell wanted to take us all on," Sansing said evenly. "He made his choice, thinking he could get away with it. But he's not going to." He walked over to her table and stood there and finally she looked up at him. "I want to arrest him. Do you understand that? I mean to put him in jail and bring him to trial for killing the Harms boy. The jury will decide the rest."

"You're lying," she said. "You hope that killer across the street gets him."

"Rand will stay out of this," Sansing said.

"Will he?" She laughed without humor.

Sansing turned and went to the front window and looked across the street, but Rand was no longer standing in front of the hotel. He frowned a

182

moment, then said, "Somewhere, along that street, in a dark place, Purcell's waiting to kill you, Jim. I can't ask you to make a target of yourself."

"I'm not goin' to stay in here," Cardigan said. He laid the rifle on one of the tables and went behind the bar for the sawed-off shotgun. He broke it open, checked the loads, then closed it. "I think I'd better settle this with Smoke."

"Not alone," Sansing said. "We'll search the street, on both sides. And I'll stand for no arguments." He turned to the door and stood there, then he looked toward the hotel and saw that Rand was back at his post, leaning against the hitching rack. "I would say," Sansing murmured, "that Rand's been pointing Purcell out to us all the time, only we weren't smart enough to see it."

Cardigan and Staffen came up and stood behind the sheriff and looked at Rand, blocked by the deep shadows of the street. "Sure," Staffen said. "Purcell's along this street somewhere. That's why Rand's facing this way."

"We'll cross over together," Sansing said, "and go along the walk. When we spot him, we'll fan out and try to take him without any shooting."

Lila Ramey laughed. "What you mean is that you'll drive him out so that Rand gets his shot."

Sansing looked at her. "That's not what I mean and you know it." He pushed open the door and stepped out, paused a moment until they were together, then they all walked rapidly across the street.

Sansing led them south and they stayed close to the buildings and kept watching the other side, paying particular attention to the dark gaps between the buildings. They were edgy, cautious men, ready to jump at the first shot, the first movement, for they were at a disadvantage; Purcell was probably watching every step they took.

Cardigan said, "It's me he wants. Let me go ahead."

"We stay together," Sansing said flatly. "Damn it, I won't tell you again."

"Then don't," Cardigan said and in three jumps he gained the center of the street, swinging his head first one way and then the other, waiting for Purcell to take the first shot. Out of the corner of his eye he saw Rand come alive and swing toward him and Cardigan whirled, thinking that Rand had spotted Purcell somewhere behind him, but he saw nothing.

There was a shot, heavy-sounding, from a big-bore rifle, and he wheeled around again and saw Rand fall. Sansing and Staffen ran out into the street, ready to take up the shooting, but there were no more shots fired.

For a moment they stood there, wondering where that one shot had come from, then the saloon door opened and Lila Ramey stepped out, holding the rifle Cardigan had laid on the bar.

She said, "Did you think I'd stand by and let him be murdered?"

184

Bert Staffen ran back to Rand and rolled him over, then his shout split the silence of the street. "Val! Jim!"

They came up and saw what had excited Staffen. Smoke Purcell looked up at them with dead, wide-open eyes, an expression of complete surprise on his face; the bullet had taken him high in the chest and passed clean through him. Staffen quickly crossed the walk and searched in the gap between the buildings, then he dragged Rand out, and when Lila Ramey saw this she rushed across the street and threw herself on Purcell. She screamed and then her voice became a bubbling wail.

Sansing was putting it together. He said, "When we were inside the saloon, Purcell sneaked around behind Rand and belted him with a gun barrel then swapped clothes with him and took his place." He looked at Cardigan. "He was going to cut you down when Lila shot from the saloon, thinking that Rand had spotted Purcell and was about to cut him down with the shotgun." He stepped over and lifted Lila and had to tear her hands away from Purcell's body to do it.

She had a wildness in her eyes and shouted, "I loved him! He was going to give me everything!"

"No man has everything," Sansing said. He saw Helen Jensen and the bartender standing back and nodded to them and they came up. "Take her up to the doctor's and he can give her something to quiet her."

185

The shot had wakened the town and lamps were being lit and a few men appeared on the street, nightshirts tucked into their pants.

Rand moaned and tried to sit up and Cardigan and Staffen helped him up; he stood there, reeling and rubbing the back of his head. Val Sansing said, "Take him inside the saloon and pour a drink in him." He turned to the gathering crowd and fended them off and the three men crossed to the saloon. Sansing came in a few minutes later. Pete Manning had not moved from his chair. Rand was at the bar, leaning heavily against it, a bottle and glass in front of him.

The sheriff sided him and said, "You came in here on the train. I don't think you ought to wait for one out. My horse is tied out front. Get on it and keep going."

Rand slowly raised his head and looked at Sansing, then he nodded and tossed off another drink. "I suppose news of this will get around. That's how a man's reputation gets damaged."

"What reputation?" Sansing asked. "Rand, no one cares enough about you to talk about you, one way or another. Now get the hell out of this county."

"All right," Rand said and turned to the door. He stopped there and looked at Pete Manning. "Sorry. It was the way the cards fell."

"Sure," Manning said. "We can't win 'em all."

Rand went out and before the door could close,

Helen Jensen and the bartender stepped inside; they looked at Rand as he mounted up, but said nothing.

Jim Cardigan stood there, then he walked over to Pete Manning and swept the cards to the floor. "The game's over, friend."

Manning looked at the cards in the sawdust and said, "And I was going to win that too."

"You just thought you was," Cardigan said. "I've got a dislike for a man who don't fight his own fights. Go find yourself another town."

Manning looked at him, then at Val Sansing, and said, "Are you going to stand there and let him talk to me like that?"

"I'll hold his coat while he kicks the hell out of you," Sansing said.

"Now wait a minute," Manning said, rising.

"That's all the time you've got," Cardigan said. "Do what you want to do."

There was a hesitation in Manning, but it was brief. "I'm not going to die for nothing," he said and buttoned his coat. "I've got some packing and . . ."

"Be on the morning train," Sansing said. He stood there and waited, then Manning nodded and went out, slamming the door.

Jim Cardigan walked behind the bar and set out a bottle and a water glass. He said, "By the time that's down to the label, I usually start singin', but tonight maybe I'll just cry a little." He uncorked it and poured the glass full, then stood there and looked at it. "He was never easy to understand, you know. Kind of moody. But he was a good kid. Everybody used to say so." He looked at Sansing and Bert Staffen. "What am I going to do now that he's gone? I came here because of him. Don't I ever have any reasons of my own for doin' a thing?" He picked up the glass and raised it, but before it touched his lips, he stopped and held it that way, then flung the glass across the room. "Do I need that slop? Can't I ever take my troubles cold sober?"

Helen Jensen came in from the street in time to hear him. She stepped up to the bar and took the bottle and put it aside. "Jim, you don't need that. You did the best you could and it's not your fault that it wasn't enough."

"How do I know that?"

"You don't. We never really do, but we have to believe that."

He nodded. "What about Lila? What happens to her?"

"I don't know," Helen said. "But at least one of her problems is solved because she has lost the baby. Doc's put her to sleep over at the hotel. Maybe it'll turn out lucky for her she lost Smoke too. Jim, we never know what's going to happen. We just live and do our best and hope it comes out good."

Cardigan looked at Bert Staffen. "Is that so, Bert?"

"That's about it," Staffen said. "Jim, stay here now. Don't get it into your head to go off someplace. I need you at the store. Helen needs you. Hell, man, we've all got a lot of work to do here. Purcell's left a mess and it has got to be cleaned up. The bank's in this with a good-sized loan and they'll want to clear out of it. It'll take a good man to get it straightened out so that Means and the others don't get hurt any more. Jim, you could do that job. I want you to do it."

"If you think they'd . . ."

"They'd want that," Val Sansing said. "I agree with Bert."

He was touched by this faith, this trust, and he stood there, head down, thinking it over. "I guess," he said, "it's the right thing. I always wanted to do the right thing." Then he shrugged off his dark thoughts and smiled. "It's kind of amusin' because a marshal ran me out of another town and now you folks are askin' me to stay." He shook his head. "It was Smoke they always wanted, and not me."

"Those people didn't see too well," Staffen said.

"They saw all right," Cardigan said.

"We never see it all," Sansing said. "Bert, you want to help me carry Purcell up to the doctor's office?" He looked at Helen Jensen and smiled. Be smart now and hang onto Jim, will you?" He went out and Bert Staffen followed him. Purcell was still stretched out in the street and a few men

189

stood nearby, waiting to see what was going to happen next. "If the girl hadn't made the mistake," Sansing said, "we'd . . ."

"But she made it," Bert Staffen said. "We all make 'em, Val. Purcell made his biggest one when he let trouble come between him and Jim Cardigan. There's a man who'd stay the whole distance, Val. Right or wrong, he'd stay."

"Yes," Sansing said and turned and looked back at the saloon. "I always worried about her growing old in that place. It seemed such a shame." Then he sighed. "Well, let's get him up the stairs so I can get some sleep." He bent and lifted Purcell by the shoulders and Bert Staffen took the feet. As they crossed the walk, Sansing said, "He doesn't weigh much, does he?"

"It's life that makes a man heavy," Staffen said.

They carried him up the stairs and the watchers standing there in the street went home. When the two men came down, the town was deserted, except for the lights in the saloon, then these went out too, one by one.

Center Point Large Print
600 Brooks Road / PO Box 1
Thorndike, ME 04986-0001 USA

(207) 568-3717

US & Canada:
1 800 929-9108
www.centerpointlargeprint.com